Thrilling Adventures

Edited by R. Edgewood

Published by 53rd Street Publishing

Offices in Gibsons, B.C. Canada and Lincoln City, Oregon

Other collections and anthologies by the author

Tales of Urban Fantasy
Tales of Bizarre Detectives
Tales of Mystery and Suspense
Tales of Weird Fantasy
Tales of Twisted Crime
Tales of The Unexpected
Tales From Space
10 by Russ Crossley
Round Up At The Burger Bar: The Story of Trixie Pug,
Parts 1- 5 The Beginning
Worlds of Science Fiction and Fantasy
More Tales of Mystery and Suspense
Justice Served
Love Stories
Ladies of the Jolly Roger
The Adventures of Razor and Edge:
An Unexpected Journey
On Edge
Thrilling Adventures
Total War

Don't you hate when the engines of your plane stop at 30,000 feet?

The steady thrumming of the engines died away. Ellen's heart leapt to her throat and she swallowed a scream.

Oh, God, no. I'm going to die...

She became weightless as the plane began to drop rapidly, losing altitude at an ever-increasing rate. The seat belt dug into her flesh, making her grimace in pain. Closing her eyes, Ellen said a silent prayer, her hands gripping the seat arms. As the aircraft's speed steadily increased, her seat belt struggled to keep her from flying upward into the ceiling.

Puffing her cheeks, she attempted to suck in air—but the seatbelt tightened around her waist making breathing seem impossible. Her thoughts became muddled and foggy as her mind drifted to her ex-husband and the love they once shared. She hoped she'd be unconscious before the plane crashed. Her mother had died such an agonizingly slow death from bone cancer; Ellen wanted a quick exit.

This might be her time. "I'm so sorry, Albert...really..." she whispered.

"I love you, Mom."

Acknowledgments

Thank you to our editor, Colleen Kuehne, for her diligent work to improve our work. We are forever grateful to her. And to all those authors who inspired the book you have in your hands. Thank you all for your wonderful, thrilling stories.

Dedication

For the fans who shares our love of the fantastic.

Thrilling Adventures

Edited by R. Edgewood

Published by 53rd Street Publishing

Cover art © Sandra Iacone | Dreamstime
Cover designed by R. Edgewood
Cover design and layout © 2015 by 53rd Street Publishing

Print ISBN: 978-1-927621-42-4
53rd Street Publishing
Head office: Gibsons B.C. Canada
www.53rdstreetpublishing.com

Table of Contents

Introduction

About the Author

Another title available from 53rd Street Publishing

Introduction

I have been a fan of science fiction and fantasy since I began reading. The stories that thrilled me and held—and still do—the most interest for me contain action paired with fantastic ideas. Reading pulse pounding tales bring me great joy and excitement.

These selected tales offer the same sense of excitement that thrilled me all those years ago and I hope will do the same for you.

Enjoy!

R. Edgewood

August 2015

Steampunk is a unique milieu for storytelling. This tale set in a steampunk alternate history where the outcome of a race between two rivals will determine the fate of an empire.

The Great Bicycle Race

MASTER COPPERWAITE BURST INTO THE DUSTY WORKSHOP scattering puffs of soot into the small workshop kept warm by the fire in the coal-fueled smelter in one corner of the room. "Phillip! Why aren't you working? You know we have to finish the steam cycle for the Crown Prince today." The heavy door bumped the edge of the worktable running the length of one wall. The solid oak door separated the customer reception of The Copperwaite Bicycle Emporium (est. 1788) from the workshop where Phillip created the magic. Literally.

The sudden intrusion startled Phillip out of his daydreaming. He'd been watching the comings and goings of everyday life from the workshop window facing busy Covent Road.

The road was busy with the horse drawn carriages driven by men with top hats the color of coal dust, the sidewalks teamed with unescorted ladies with their intricate hairdos flowing from beneath bonnets of all shapes, colors, and sizes, and their billowing spring dresses were decorated with multi-colored ribbons.

Now that they enjoyed the vote women had become free to walk the streets without the company of a male companion.

Phillip approved of the new Victorian woman; many of his sex did not. Including Mr. Copperwaite. No doubt his daughter Penny's liberal attitude irked her father's old ways.

Life in London went by this window every day while Phillip Host toiled in the shop building bicycles. Sometimes he just had to stop to enjoy his newfound home.

Normally rainy, London had given way to spring, bright sunshine encouraging new life in Her Royal Highnesses kingdom. High overhead a magnificent azure sky, dotted with puffy white clouds reminding him of fluffy cotton candy sold during the summer fair, added to the beauty of the day. His mouth watered at the memory of the sweet treat. But duty called shoving from his mind all other considerations.

I have a job to do; the Empire is depending on me.

Phillip stared back unable to comprehend Mr. Copperwaite's words, his fleshy, round face was as red as a summer apple. He glared at Phillip with hazel-gray eyes so intense it sent a tremor of fear through him. His employer could be a scary man.

Did he say we needed to finish a bicycle? He must mean me, there is no we in bicycle. "Sorry, Master Copperwaite, I will have the bicycle ready on time as promised."

Mr. Copperwaite is a middle-aged man with wide, snow-white sideburns. At the shop he always wears a knee length leather apron covering his gray work shirt and matching pants. A pair of riding goggles with darkened lenses sat high on his forehead the strap tight about his mostly bald scalp. No doubt he'd been demonstrating the latest model steam cycle Phillip built to a customer.

He emitted a grunt of disapproval then slammed the door leaving Phillip alone once again.

Six months after arriving in London, Phillip Host, alchemist and inventor, built the first nuclear fusion steam driven cycle designed to travel faster than a horse drawn carriage at full gallop. The new technology made Copperwaite's small shop busier, and Phillips new designs in higher demand, than in the history of the family owned business.

Phillip however refused to share the secrets behind his revolutionary innovations with anyone, even Mr. Copperwaite, no matter how much money he was offered. Mr. Copperwaite threatened to fire him unless he revealed the secret, but Phillip knew he couldn't or lose access to the revolutionary designs.

The truth was Phillip feared the shards of mineral he used to generate the force shield to protect the rider from the radiation produced by the engine would misused by zealots for some nefarious purpose. The shards he derived from a stone inset into an amulet left him by his mentor after he died. At first he'd been reluctant to cannibalize the amulet but had no choice for now, at least until he made his own fortune. Mr. Copperwaite had been kind enough to give him a job when he first came to London so he owed the man for his kindness.

Many of the ancient alchemy texts said transmutation of common elements was possible but he hadn't yet found the ancient formula.

The number of alchemy artists, and the corresponding number of related ancient texts available, were greater in London than anywhere in the industrialized world so the ultimate secret had to be here or it was more myth than truth.

The bicycle design and building business paid the bills until he reached the pinnacle of alchemist society by demonstrating a powerful new invention he'd been thinking about that would change the world. The steam bicycle was a decent invention, rather simple really, but it did serve to attract attention to his skills.

London based alchemist's legitimized alchemy in the minds of the government when they eliminated the coal smoke that nearly made the city uninhabitable only ten years ago. An invention this dramatic demonstrated true skill of the alchemist and drew a lot of attention making any practitioner of the craft respected in government circles and celebrated in the alchemy community.

Convincing commoners alchemy wasn't black magic was another matter entirely. In the past five years a number of anti-alchemy clubs had sprung up across the city, their members demanding all alchemists be banished. So far the government had resisted their efforts citing the good acts of many practitioners of the art.

Cries for censure increased when an evil alchemist, Dr. Sam Acorn, allegedly used his magic arts to generate the flash flooding of the Thames River killing several thousand people in 1881.

Then there were the persistent rumors linking Sam to the coup attempt by rebel British army officers in 1883 that killed many more people, and resulted in the murder of Prime Minister Lord Churchill. Some even speculated Sam provided support for the German Kiser's successful invasion of Ireland in 1885.

But no direct connection has ever been established between Sam and these events hence no criminal charges have ever been filed.

When the dark alchemist disappeared four years ago the Brotherhood of Alchemists struck his name from their membership rolls, the first practitioner ejected from the organization in the past thousand years.

Sam's books were confiscated and were now in the Brotherhoods members' only library, under lock and key since the books were rumored to contain dark spells and formulas, which had the potential to destroy the world.

Phillip considered the rumors an exaggeration by some of Sam' supporters of which there were many. But if Sam were so evil he certainly would have used the extreme spells by now. However, Phillip also knew whatever books of Sam' were in the library they would have to contain dangerous information or the Brotherhood wouldn't have restricted access. Overly cautious men and women may lead the Brotherhood but they weren't fools.

Phillip looked at the partially completed bicycle's sleek lines and low profile the frame secured in the steel scaffolding he'd constructed specifically to hold a bicycle frame while he worked. The frame itself was a made from single piece of hybrid carbon steel lighter than any metal manufactured in the past hundred years. Anyone duplicating his invention would have to pay him a very high fee. So far no one had used his invention however he was confident with the recent advances in technology; the aero-plane and auto-mobile companies would soon be lining up to pay him great wads of currency. Until then he would remain working for Mr. Copperwaite.

The shielded housing containing the steam generator sat perched behind the riders seat welded to a steel guard above the tire to keep them from rubbing.

The housing was about six inches long, round like a large cigar, and he had pasted a yellow warning label on it instructing the rider never to tamper with the housing or risk certain death.

Phillip sighed and walked to the bicycle in progress to begin his work again. He had been delaying the inevitable too long already.

He screwed the on switch into the housing and the bicycle was complete. Flicking the switch the steam generator came on and the motor attached by hinged arms on either side to the rear wheel began to hum. All would be needed now was to use the gearshift lever on the horizontal handle bar to shift into go and the rider would be off. In this case the rider being Crown Prince Bertrum, heir to the throne of England, Scotland, and the half of Wales not ceded to the Dutch after the War of The Tulips.

The smells of steam and axel greased filled Phillip's senses as the hum increased. The motor gradually gained strength.

Suddenly the door to the reception area burst open and the Crown Prince dressed in a powered blue suit carrying an ivory handled walking stick entered. The door slammed shut behind him. He pulled up as he saw the completed bicycle his muddy brown eyes intense.

"Phillip. It's beautiful." His royal highness, his voice a low whisper said as he gaped at his newest acquisition. The Prince smoothed his shirt with the flat of one long fingered hand as he set his walking stick next to the smelter.

"What do you call it?"

"A steam cycle, Majesty."

"Ah, yes, very appropriate. I approve."

Good for you, thought Phillip.

The prince circled the steam cycle, his eyes traveling the length and breath of the steel and exotic metals it was made of while it continued to hum with power. His eyes burned with the intensity only a manic personality could produce. His smile became wider with each step forward.

Finally he stopped then turned to face Phillip, his eyes brimming with wonder his thick body trembling. "Now the real test begins," he said gleefully.

"Sorry, Majesty, what test?"

Prince Bert, as the Fleet Street papers referred to the Crown Prince, had all sorts of loony ideas so Phillip immediately regretted asking the question. Whatever tests the Prince had dreamed up had to be something dangerous or stupid, but Phillip had no choice but to agree.

The British Loyalty Act of 1878 reinstated the royal authority to have a subject's head chopped off for the least infraction. Of course no member of the royal family had exercised this authority, but Prince Bert was so bug-slapped-nuts he just might lop off a few heads and Phillip didn't wish to be the first in line.

"Why the race, naturally." The prince slapped Phillip's chest gently with the back of his hand then once again circled the bicycle his eyes intent on every detail.

Race? What race? Phillip rolled his eyes. He knew befriending a crazy bastard would come back to haunt him sooner than later. Fearing the answer he waited, his guts twisting for the Prince to elaborate.

After several agonizing minutes passed he opened his mouth to speak when Bert suddenly added, "You will beat him of this much I'm certain."

"Beat whom, Majesty?"

"Samuel Gesture." He threw his arms out wide almost hitting Phillip who managed to step back before the Prince's arm made contact. "Your steam cycle is the fastest, sleekest, most powerful in the competition. Britain will rule the road just as it once did the waves."

Dropping his arms to his sides he retrieved his walking stick then turned to face Phillip. Taking a step toward him he stabbed an index finger into Phillip's chest causing him to wince. "You will be triumphant for the glory of the Empire." With those words the Prince turned his back to him then headed for the door to reception.

Phillips' mind reeled in confusion. Sam? A race? What the hell is this lunatic talking about? Everyone knew Sam gesture was the most decorated cyclist in the world. Phillip had no chance of winning. "But, Majesty, where and when is this race?"

The Prince stopped and without turning around he said, "Mr. Copperwaite has the details. Don't forget, Phillip, you will win. Or suffer the consequences," he added before Prince Bert threw open the door and exited the workshop. Phillip stood unmoving alone once again.

Phillip didn't move or speak for several minutes; the only sounds being the hum of the still running bicycle and the soft roar of the coal burning in the smelter.

"I may to have to flee the Empire," he finally murmured under his breath. Instinctively his hand went to his throat.

***

Phillips riding goggles filtered the bright sunshine coming from the cloudless blue sky so he could see the meandering road cut through the green parkland.

Sparrows and finches chirped from the branches of pine and oak trees dotting the perfectly manicured lawns of the Gray family estate as he brought the steam cycle to a stop on the circular driveway of the old house.

Situated in the small village of Wembley at the edge of London, the house and lands had been once owned by Sir John Gray, a wealthy London merchant. The property had been willed to the village after Sir John's death and had since been converted into parkland with the house used for concerts and receptions.

Today though the estate would be the starting point of The Great Bicycle Race to South Hampton. The winner's design would be awarded a contract with the British Army of five thousand bicycles for use by a newly formed top-secret unit of the army. And, most importantly to Phillip, the winning rider would gain unlimited access to the secret books in the Brotherhood's members-only library.

According to Phillip's informant (a wantabe alchemist named Jack he'd been tutoring) in the army quartermaster's office this top-secret units mission is covert operations at the behest of Queen Victoria. Jack refused to share further details but Phillip sensed the contract was a priority for the government. And a priority for his survival.

Sam represented the German Empire and their recent industrial advances in the fields of propulsion and weapons development. They wanted to win the race to demonstrate to the world how the sun had set on the British Empire. Phillip suspected the Germans were never interested in the British contract since they had been posturing for war since the rise to power of their dynamic chancellor, Otto von Bismarck.

Of course the German Foreign Minister, Von Schelling, denied this to the press claiming he eagerly waited to place his signature alongside Prime Minister Wellington's on the contract.

Just as Phillip's steam cycle rolled to a stop and disengaged the motor Sam pulled up alongside astride a bicycle that took Phillip's breath away.

Phillip sucked in a breath when he recognized the frame of Sam's' cycle was made of his patented hybrid carbon steel. Regardless the sky blue and tomato red bicycle was the sleekest, most beautiful machine Phillip had ever seen.

Sam sat up straight after letting go of the handle bar controls using his gloved hands to lift his goggles from his eyes. The seat was thickly padded seat with a high back, and behind the rider was a fuel tank and a bell-shaped nozzle extending off the end of the fender Phillip recognized being for a rocket exhaust. Phillip detected the smell of burnt carbon coming from Sam's direction.

Phillip's cheeks were suddenly cooler than they should in the warm spring sunshine. Somehow Sam had invented the rocket-propelled bicycle, something thought impossible by most scientists, alchemists, and Phillip. And Sam had stolen his patented steel to construct his machine.

He swallowed hard but his mouth tasted dry and metallic. I'm in big trouble.

"Hello, Sam, it's been a long time." In truth they'd never met.

The champion dismounted then shifted his gaze to Phillip. He cocked one oil black eyebrow as a humorless smile passed across his swarthy features. His black hair slicked back by oil and his black suit added to his mysterious, dangerous appearance.

"Phillip Host isn't it?" Phillip nodded. Sam let go of his bicycle and stepped away from it.

Phillip gaped at the machine then at Sam who had a wicked grin on his face.

"How...?"

"Force field," explained Sam. "Impressive don't you think?" Phillip gave only a slight nod in response. Sam chuckled then walked away toward the German foreign minster who had called to him to join him at the official ceremony.

Suddenly snapped from his stupor, Phillip draped his gloves, goggles, and helmet on the seat of his steam bicycle then hurried to join Mr. Copperwaite and his daughter, Penny.

When he arrived at his seat Penny's hair the color of glowed in the bright sunshine. Prince Bert was seated the other side of Penny Copperwaite facing the speaker's platform. Overhead German and British flags flapped in the breeze alongside the Brotherhoods flag. Queen Victoria would speak first, then the British Prime Minister, and then the race would begin. The Crown Prince would fire the starting pistol to start the race to South Hampton. Phillip hoped the gun wasn't aimed at him at the time.

Once seated beside his employer, Phillip leaned closer to his ear so his words wouldn't be overheard. "Sir, I'm going to lose the race—"

Mr. Copperwaite turned sharply in his seat silencing him with a glare, his jaw tight, and his fists clenched. "The word lose does exist in my dictionary. Are we clear?"

"Uhhh, yes...sir." Phillip swallowed his words.

Uncertain, Phillip once again leaned toward his employer's ear. "Sir, is something wrong?"

"I had to agree to arrange for my daughter marry Dr. Acorn should he win the race." He glared at Phillip. "Don't let me down."

He faced forward just the Queen rose to speak.

Phillip swallowed hard and his heart beat faster. Damn, I'm in a fix.

***

Now astride his bicycle the sound of his heart pounding in his ears covering the hum of the steam engine behind him. Phillip had his tinted goggles covering his eyes and the fingers inside his leather gloves hovered over the shifter on the handle bar. Stealing a glance to his right he saw Sam' sleek bicycle with the swept back frame looked much faster than his machine. The vibration of the running rocket motor attached to Sam' machine passed through his lean frame in waves of energy. He swallowed hard and waited for the starters shot.

Shifting to look at the speaker's platform he saw the round smiling face of the Crown Prince who appeared very pleased with himself. The Prince raised the pistol over his head, the barrel pointing at the clear blue sky.

On the count of three the Prince closed his eyes and squeezed off a single shot and they were off.

Immediately Sam's rocket bicycle shot forward and he instantly had a substantial lead speeding to the edge of the parkland surrounding the estate where a service road disappeared into the trees.

Panicking, his heart racing, Phillip stabbed at the shift lever and accidentally shifted the steam cycle into reverse. His hands straining under the force of gravity as the powerful bike leapt backward like a bucking bronco forcing him to grip the handlebars as tight as possible. Finally he managed to shift into neutral again.

The steam cycle came to an abrupt halt and he managed not to be thrown over the handlebars.

His cheeks puffing in and out, perspiration running down his face, he paused to gather himself and calm down. Slowly his heart rate eased and he straightened his shoulders sitting higher in the seat. Looking down he touched the shift handle and slipped it into gear in the GO position.

The steam cycle started moving forward slowly gathering speed. A quick glance at the speakers platform confirmed Mr. Copperwaite, the Crown Prince, even the Queen, were cheering him forward.

I must be doing well. Peering ahead he saw Sam had already disappeared into the trees. Looking at the speed indicator dial he saw the steam cycle was travelling faster than he thought he'd designed it to go.

How is this possible? Pushing any remaining doubts from his mind Phillip leaned forward on the seat making his profile smaller and pressed the speed lever forward until it would go no further. His confidence grew as each mile came and went. The smells of the road were like intoxicating, the startled cows as he sped past country farms, the whining horses dumping their riders then bolting across the meadows beside the dirt road. All of it thrilled him to the core of his being.

The wind whipped at him as he rode. After inadvertently swallowing an unidentified insect left a bitter taste in his mouth he remembered to keep his mouth shut.

Since South Hampton was located eighty-three miles from London and his speed indicator showed he was traveling at fifty-two miles per hour.

According to his calculations, barring of course the unexpected, if he maintained this rate of speed he would arrive at South Hampton in one hour, thirty-nine point six minutes from his time of departure. Pulling out his pocket watch from his vest pocket he stole a quick look before putting it away. He would be there in twenty-four minutes from now.

Filled with a burst of renewed determination a small smile paled across his lips then he glared straight ahead and leaned ever lower, the wind howled in his ears louder.

Suddenly the unexpected appeared at the side of the road. A large swath of the road looked like it had been on fire. The soil, the grasses at the edges were black as soot. Also a tell tale tail of smoke rose from the irrigation ditch. Phillip had a bad feeling about this.

He gradually slowed until finally coming to a stop next to the blackened ditch. Someone may be seriously hurt. I need to help if I can.

A field of tall wild grasses rose beyond the ditch disappearing to the horizon until they met a forest of trees.

Lifting his goggles from his eyes Phillip peered into the ditch but still couldn't see anything. He dismounted after setting the bike on its kickstand then strode to the edge to get a better look.

His heart sank he realized what had happened. There in the bottom of the ditch was the twisted blackened ruin of Sam's rocket bicycle. The fire after what had obviously been an explosion had gone out but not before the vehicle had been destroyed. But where was Sam?

From somewhere in the tall grass beyond Phillip heard a groan and a soft cry for help. After draping his goggles over the handle bar on his bike he doffed his coat and vest and struggled across the ditch into the field of wild grass.

Following the sounds he finally found a bloody, soot covered Sam laying on his back his arms at his sides. His eyes were open but he blinked them rapidly over and over. He gasped for breath and Phillip sensed the evil inventor wasn't long for this world. Phillip knelt in the grass next to the dying alchemist.

Sam coughed ejecting blood from the sides of his mouth. "Phillip, is that you?" The alchemists voice was harsh and ragged and he winced since he was in obvious pain.

"Yes, Sam, it's me," he said softly.

"Phillip...Phil...take care of...books...transmutation..." Unable to continue Sam coughed violently then shuddered as his breath escaped from his lips for the final time and his body relaxed. His eyes remained open and sightless, the spark of life gone.

Easing back on his haunches Phillip sighed. Sam was dead. Now all he had to do to win was finish the ride to South Hampton and the books would be his. As he'd hoped with those secrets he would finally create his ultimate invention, a flying auto-mobile to revolutionize the air and compete with the birds.

Standing he walked away but stopped to steal one last look at his adversary's dead body to remind himself of the terrible price paid for advances in science and magic. Phillip then went back to his steam cycle and rode away feeling sorry for Sam. Though the man was an evil alchemist he didn't deserve to die by his own invention. A working rocket cycle was a remarkable accomplishment, if it worked.

Soon the finish line, a man standing beside the mustard yellow ribbon stretched across the road, holding megaphone waved to the crowd indicating he'd seen the steam cycle's approach.

As Phillip rode within earshot the man raised the megaphone to his mouth and shouted, "Ladies, gentlemen, boys and girls, please give a warm welcome to first of those brave young men on their astounding bicycles!" The echo of the crowds roars and clapping swept over him as he came closer.

The man must have recognized became his voice became excited and he began to jump up and down. "Our first arrival is the pride of the British Empire, Phillip Host!"

Now the crowd surged toward the finish line and small British flags appeared in many people's hands. Somewhere a brass band began to play Britannia Rules the Waves.

Phillip swallowed his growing fear of the large crowd that seemed an endless sea of heads, hats, and flags.

Finally he drove through the ribbon parting it in two and came to a stop next to the man with the megaphone. His bowler hat, handle bar mustache, and plaid jacket made Phillip think the man's occupation was as a carnival barker, which he very well may be.

The man stepped up to greet him using one hand to slap his back hard jarring Phillip. "Hello, lad, welcome to South Hampton." In all the noise of the hiss of the steam engine, overlapping voices, shouts, and the music the man had to shout to be heard.

Phillip turned off his bike then slipped off one riding glove so he could remove his goggles, which he raised to his hairline on his forehead. He smiled.

"Thank you, sir."

"The Queen's party will be arriving shortly. Please follow me to the race manager's table so he can record your time."

Phillip nodded then dismounted and pushed his bike after the man through the parkland past the crowd of well wishers who slapped his back and shouted things like,

16

"Jolly good! For the glory of the Empire! Well done, old boy!"

Food and drink vendors dotted the park filling the air with the smells of sweet and savory foods, cooked meats, fried dough, and other treats. The scene was exactly what he feared it would become, a circus. He had been used. It made him wonder if Sam' bike had been sabotaged.

No one had asked him about the other rider. Maybe the race manager would ask about Sam, if he didn't then he knew something would be very rotten in South Hampton.

With a nod of his head the man indicated the race managers table. Phillip walked his bike to the table and stopped. The man seated behind the table was rail thin, wearing a black suit such as those worn by undertakers, and his wire rimmed spectacles sat near the end of his long nose.

"Phillip Host?" he asked his voice reedy.

"Yes."

"British I presume?" Phillip nodded.

The corners of his bloodless lips curled up slightly. "Excellent." Looking at a gold pocket watch from his vest pocket he recorded the time in an open ledger on the table in front of him. "William will show you the reception area."

Phillip assumed he was dismissed. Feeling a little bewildered he followed William, who turned out to be the man from the finish line, to a reception area identical to the one at Wembly. The flags, the speakers' platform and podium everything was in place just as they were at the start line. The only thing missing was the dignitaries.

Armed British soldiers, wearing their dress uniforms, were stationed at the perimeter of the seating area. They admitted him without any trouble so he strode to the front row and sat down.

Phillip was grateful he was alone. He needed time to think. He won the race, what else mattered? He winced inside at the thought. He had integrity.

"Phillip, as I live and breath," said a familiar voice from behind him.

Looking over his shoulder he saw the smiling Prince Bert approaching from behind using the aisle between the rows of chairs set up for the reception. Phillip cringed inside and turned to face forward.

"You're the winner! Congratulations!" The Prince sat in an empty chair next to him and slapped his back.

"Highness," began Phillip uncertain at first if he should ask but quickly throwing caution to the wind since he was the celebrated winner of the race. He looked into the Princes eyes. "Did someone sabotage Sam' bicycle?"

The smile on the Prince's face faded and his eyes hardened. He lowered his voice as he spoke. "Of course, lad, for the good of the Empire you had to win. We could not taker any chances." He patted Phillip's arm with the flat of one hand. "I'm sure you concur."

Suddenly the Prince leapt to his feet the smile once again wide on his face. "Momsie, will be here shortly. You'll receive the Order of the British Empire and be the grandest alchemist in all the land. It will be glorious!" With those final words Prince Bert hurried off disappearing from view behind the speakers platform.

Phillip's body sagged and he closed his eyes. Grand was not the word he would he used to describe himself right now. He had nothing to do with the sabotage, but the entire affair was a fraud.

Everyone would be happy except him. He'd have the books, and maybe Penny, but he'd know it was all a massive fraud. No. He could not abide such a thing.

He decided to leave not only London but also England. He'd always wanted to seek warmer climes, witness first hand dancing girls in grass skirts, swim in warm blue seas teaming with colorful fish. Paradise awaited him. His life as an alchemist was over.

Jumping to his feet he ran to his steam bike. The bike would no doubt only take him as far as the docks in South Hampton before the mineral was exhausted, but that would be enough for him to find a ship. He'd use his remaining funds to pay for passage to the South Pacific.

The steam bike would be useless without the magic mineral so he didn't have to worry about it being used for nefarious purposes.

His heart sang as he set off for the docks the hum and hiss of the steam cycle's engine filling his hearing blocking out the yelling behind him.

He knew not whatever adventure life held for him next, but he was certain his new life would be exciting.

*Stories about Area 51 and the early atomic experiments in the
Nevada desert have always intrigued me. Tales concerning aliens
and atomic weapons goes back to the earliest days of science fiction.
This story provides the connection.*

Survivors

May 5, 1955

Nevada Test Site - Operation Teapot - Test Apple-2

THOUGH HE WAS WEARING PROTECTIVE GOGGLES—he had been
assured the dark lenses would protect his eyes—Lieutenant JG
Edward Dugan still averted his eyes when a flash as bright as the
sun lit up the early morning sky over the test site. When he crouched
below the bunker wall, he pressed his trembling hand against the
cool steel that was two feet thick and covered by earth. The steel was
becoming warmer with each passing second.

The hushed voices of the senior officers and scientists around
him helped to keep his fear buried. They didn't sound afraid as
he was, only more in awe of the force of the blast created by the
exploded atom bomb.

A faint taste of acidic bile from the back of Edward's throat
and his heart pounding against his ribs reminded him he was still
alive.

"Quite a show, eh, Dugan?"

Edward glanced to his right to see General Marks peering through the slit opening along one bunker wall, his binoculars trained on the blast site. The bunker windows were made of special glass. In order to stop the radiation. The glass was made with a mixture consisting of twenty six percent lead. The viewing window was inches thick sufficient to protect anyone looking out through the slit from flying debris.

The general dropped to his haunches as the roar of the blast wave swept over the bunker like a vengeful, super-heated spirit. High-speed winds peppered the bunker with rocks and dirt.

Though he'd never experienced actual combat, Edward imagined the sound was like being attacked by enemy machine guns.

A loud *thud* announced the arrival of debris from Survival Town, the artificial town specifically constructed for the test.

General Marks offered him a lopsided grin. The oval lenses of the dark goggles glinted in the pale golden glow of the emergency lights in the ceiling of the bunker. Over six feet in height, General Marks had always seemed a giant to Edward, who stood five feet ten in his GI-issue boots.

Marks had won the Congressional Medal of Honor in Korea for leading his troops in a successful battle at Hill 402, where they routed three companies of Chinese regulars, and he had been a decorated company captain in Europe during World War II. The guy was a real-life war hero. Now as a general, he was in charge of Operation Teapot to further test atomic weapons in case they were needed against America's latest enemy: the dreaded Reds.

Edward had been too young for Korea, never mind the Second World War. His job was as General Marks' aide. The thought of using atomic weapons terrified him.

At last the howling winds waned and the rapid, pelting sounds abated.

Marks shoved his goggles up his dirt-streaked forehead, revealing his icy blue eyes; the corners wrinkled as he smiled. "Dugan," he began, "I want you to take a couple of men and go check Survival Town for me. I want a quick on-site assessment of the damage before these egg heads..."

With a slight nod of his head, he indicated the four scientists in civilian garb, huddled together in one corner of the bunker. "...are escorted into the area."

The scientists stood next to a pine table brimming with Geiger counters and other measuring devices Edward didn't recognize (and had been told the knowledge of which was well above his pay grade).

"Yes, sir." Edward was glad to be leaving the bunker. Being confined in enclosed spaces had made him uncomfortable ever since the time his older brother locked him in a closet when he was five.

Edward quickly recruited two privates, one to drive the jeep. They were soon roaring across the parched prairie toward the shattered, twisted remains of the artificial town built to assess damage from an atomic blast. Every detail had been considered.

Department stores dummies stood in for actual humans, some as children playing outside; houses were complete with furniture; even stuffed animals represented family pets. The hastily constructed houses had been set up in the town as if a sudden attack by the reds had occurred.

Edward had heard of civilians building their own survival bunkers in their backyards and basements, hoping they'd survive the war everyone expected would occur.

As the jeep bounced over the uneven landscape, Edward saw the desert had been scoured clean of cacti and scrub brush. Every living thing had been wiped away by blowing dirt and sand as if by the hand of a vengeful God. In some places there were charred plants and blackened sand, some spots shiny where the sudden burst of intense heat had turned the sand to glass. He shuddered at the thought of living people being stuck out here when a bomb such as this exploded.

Finally the jeep approached the shadows of streets of the destroyed town to find buildings collapsed in heaps of blackened wood, mannequins burned and scarred, with arms and legs gone or heads missing. They drove slowly past a children's tricycle, the frame bent and twisted; telephone poles askew at odd angles; and a speed limit sign with one corner folded back, the sign at a forty-five-degree angle, but still partially buried in the ground.

Edward swallowed hard as they passed ever-increasing damage, each more horrific than the next, until his breath caught in his throat. He stared at something that made his heart freeze. "Stop!" he shouted.

The driver stepped hard on the brake and the jeep screeched to a shuddering stop, the brakes squealing loudly.

There in the center of the town square at the junction where three streets intersected stood what appeared to be three flesh-and-blood children: one blonde girl wearing a pink party dress and two boys in dungarees and striped tee shirts, none of whom appeared to be older than ten.

They were unharmed. Their clothing bore no sign of charring, their hair was perfectly combed, not a strand out of place. They appeared to be clean, unharmed. Somehow they had survived a blast of an atomic bomb.

Edward gaped at the children, standing in a circle holding hands with their eyes closed. His mind didn't believe what his brown eyes were seeing.

Impossible.

***

May 10, 1985
Boston, Massachusetts - Julien Bar, Hotel Meridien

Ellen McKee sipped her second peach sidecar of the evening. Looking around the smoky bar, she saw that Peter and Rupert were scoping out the local talent as they did every Friday when the staff of the advertising firm of Heston, Queen, and Bradbury reconvened their meetings at Julien's after working hours.

Ellen sat alone at the table she'd been sharing with her colleagues for the past forty minutes, enjoying their initial warm-up drink of the evening together. Now was the time to prowl.

She smiled to herself as the burn of the cognac slid across her tongue, followed by the tang of the orange liqueur and lastly the sweet peach juice. She loved these weekly get-togethers. She also loved the idea of trolling for a rumpy-pumpy each week. But a good man was hard to find.

And a new man is even harder to find, she thought, scanning the predominantly male clientele and seeing the many equally recognizable and forgettable faces in the crowded bar.

Her ex-husband, Albert, would have hated the Julien Bar, with its comfortable, tanned couches and overstuffed leather chairs scattered across the hardwood floors. The stone fireplace against one wall added warmth to the dimly lit space.

A wall of mirrors, filled with shelves of liquors from all over the world, reflected the eager faces of men and women determined not go home alone, leaning on the smooth, black surface of the onyx bar in front of the mirrors many smoking cigarettes, something she'd never enjoyed.

The Julien was located in the basement of the hotel, so there were no windows.

No, Albert would have never come into such a place as this. He liked roadside bars with scarred pine tables and rickety chairs with ripped seat cushions. A spittoon and an old, mangy dog lying next to the wood-burning stove would complete Albert's dream bar.

The barrage of voices generated by the crowd of business-suited professionals spread out across the bar—some of the bar's occupants were seated on the chairs and couches, others standing in tight groups arguing, no doubt, about some sports or political big deal of the day—would have driven Albert crazy.

Maybe it was the buzz created by the alcohol, but she felt pretty good tonight. *I deserve a good time*, she thought.

She smiled into her glass. As she tipped it back to take another sip, the smell of the alcohol and juice invaded her nostrils. A light tap on her left shoulder made the lust rise from within her.

Lowering the glass, she shifted in her seat to look to her left and was startled to discover a red-haired woman dressed in a navy pantsuit and a white cotton blouse. Behind her stood a very large man with the shoulders of a Patriots linebacker, wearing a similar dark suit, only with a red tie down the front of his ivory-colored shirt. The woman's flat brown eyes gazed at her, making Ellen vaguely uncomfortable, all thoughts of sexual conquest having fled.

"Yes?" Ellen asked, her speech slightly slurred.

"Are you Ellen Thomas?"

Ellen grunted dismissively. "I used to be. I'm Ellen McKee now." Her eyes narrowed as she set her glass on the table. "What do you want?"

The woman's thin lips formed a tight smile that didn't reach her eyes. "Who says I want something?"

Ellen chuckled, her voice edged with bitterness. "In my experience, lady, *everyone* has an angle."

The woman shrugged her narrow shoulders; her suit jacket opened enough so Ellen could see a holster hidden under her jacket attached to her belt. Ellen's mouth dried and her heart skipped a beat. *Government.*

The woman reached into her jacket pocket and pulled out a black leather wallet. She flipped it open, revealing a badge and an identification card. "I'm Agent Ayres." She paused to nod at the man-mountain standing behind her, listening quietly, his features impassive, his hands folded in front of him. "This is Agent Corday. We're with the National Security Agency." The wallet disappeared in her jacket. "We'd like you to come with us."

Ellen's green eyes flitted between the two government agents. *Why are they bothering me again, after all this time?* She sighed and her shoulders slumped. "Listen, Agent Ayres, I've been questioned many times and I have nothing more I can add. I don't remember how I got there—"

"Hold on please, ma'am. I don't know what you're talking about. That information is above our pay grade. Our job is to accompany you to the airport, where a plane is waiting."

Ellen stared into Agent Ayres' eyes, trying to determine if she should believe her. Maybe, after all this time, they were going to assassinate her once she left the bar...and the others. But it didn't seem right.

Why would they bother to talk to her? Why not just take her out in an unexplained *accident?*

Of course, what worried Ellen more than dying was the plane's destination. She could refuse to go with them, only Ayres didn't actually mean they were sent to *accompany* her. Ellen knew the agents would hog-tie her if necessary and drag her to the airport.

She had no choice.

***

May 11, 1985

   Thirty thousand feet over the Nevada desert

Ellen yawned as she awoke in the enveloping comfort of the soft leather seat. She was the only passenger in a cabin that could hold twenty people. The smell of leather and men's aftershave was strong. The pilots were in the cockpit behind the door at the front of the passenger compartment. Looking down at the cup holder in the armrest of her seat, she saw her glass of vodka was gone. *Bastards took my drink.*

She smacked her lips. Her mouth tasted dry and sticky, probably due to the fifth of vodka she'd consumed last night. The corporate jet, with blackout windows, no markings on its white fuselage—other than a tail number in black and a red stripe down both sides of the plane—was well stocked with supplies for a government jet.

During the ride to the airport in a limousine—which felt more like they were at the Indy 500, they were driving so fast—Ayers kept insisting they knew nothing about the plane's final destination. (Ellen thought her partner Corday might be a robot due to his continued silence.)

Ellen thought Ayers was lying. Two armed government agents playing delivery jerks for one slightly overweight, drunken, nearly-forty-year-old woman. Their mission, to get her in a flying taxi to nowhere? It didn't make sense.

Shrugging off the question, knowing she wasn't going to get any answers by staying in Boston, Ellen boarded the plane and managed to take full advantage of the time it would take to get to wherever the plane was headed by appropriating some of the booze supply for her own personal use.

Ellen suspected the plane was headed for Groom Lake, where she'd been taken after "the event," as she called it. Somehow she'd never been able to call it the atomic bomb test, or Project Teapot, as she later learned the weapons test was called.

A violent bump jerked her forward in her seat, forcing her to hold one hand out and press it into the seat in front of her to keep from being thrown to the floor. Her stomach heaved and she burped. Her nose wrinkled as the blend of perspiration and stale booze wafted over her.

I must smell like a booze factory after an earthquake.

Glancing above her head, she saw the seatbelt light had come on, glowing red. The cabin lights suddenly went out, throwing the cabin into blackness. Her fingers cramping due to dehydration, she grabbed both ends of the seat belt and after struggling to bring them together, she finally managed to click it into place just before the aircraft suddenly tipped sharply to the left. The steady thrumming of the engines died away. Ellen's heart leapt to her throat and she swallowed a scream.

Oh, God, no. I'm going to die...

She became weightless as the plane began to drop rapidly, losing altitude at an ever-increasing rate. The seat belt dug into her flesh, making her grimace in pain. Closing her eyes, Ellen said a silent prayer, her hands gripping the seat arms. As the aircraft's speed steadily increased, her seat belt struggled to keep her from flying upward into the ceiling.

Puffing her cheeks, she attempted to suck in air—but the seatbelt tightened around her waist making breathing seem impossible. Her thoughts became muddled and foggy as her mind drifted to her ex-husband and the love they once shared. She hoped she'd be unconscious before the plane crashed. Her mother had died such an agonizingly slow death from bone cancer; Ellen wanted a quick exit. This might be her time. "I'm so sorry, Albert...really..." she whispered. "I love you, Mom."

As quickly as it started, the feeling of weightless decreased as the plane leveled off. But the engine noise hadn't returned. She opened her eyes and saw the overhead lights had come on again. What was happening?

"This is your pilot. Prepare for landing. It might be a little bumpy and we'll have to brake hard after touchdown, but don't be concerned."

Ellen thought she heard tautness in the pilot's tone that might be fear, but she decided she was imagining things. It is better not to think that the pilot of the plane you're a passenger on is as scared as you are. "You've had a stressful day," she murmured under her breath to reassure herself, then swallowed hard.

A sharp bump jarred her, then threw her upward against the seat belt, which again cut into her already painful belly flesh. She winced and held her breath. This was followed by a steadily decreasing series of bumps, the aircraft bouncing wildly beneath her.

She was tossed hard left, then hard right in her seat as the aircraft swayed side to side.

She was thrown forward when the breaks were applied, staying in her seat only because of her seat belt. In order to keep from hitting the seat in front of her, she pressed her hands into the seat back.

The screech of tires on pavement was followed by the bang of the galley doors springing open behind her and the crash of bottles, glasses, and garbage cans flinging onto the cabin floor.

Finally the plane rolled to a stop and Ellen began to breath again, sucking in deep breaths, trying to steady her heart rate back to some semblance of normal. Not that any part of this was normal.

The pilot's voice came over the cabin speaker again. "I'll be opening the doors in two minutes. Your escort has just arrived."

What, no thank you for flying Crap-Your-Pants airlines? thought Ellen.

She wondered if she should have agreed to come on this trip at all. Maybe she should have called the cops when the agents showed up. But no doubt the NSA had thought of this and had an agreement with the local cops. *They own me.*

The plane's exit door swung upward as Ellen made her way forward between the rows of seats, her low heels digging into the plush maroon carpet lining the cabin deck.

Bright sunlight streamed through the door, making her eyes water and blinding her momentarily until she blinked and brought one hand up to shade her eyes.

She stepped to the top of the ladder that extended to the cracked tarmac. A wave of heat washed over her causing beads of perspiration to immediately pop from on her upper lip and forehead. She wished now she'd brought her sunglasses.

Her vision quickly cleared. At the bottom of the stairs were two uniformed air force officers, gazing up at her. Parked behind them was an enclosed jeep with its motor still running.

The taller of the two men had steel gray hair visible around the edges of his peaked cap. She decided that he was the senior of the two officers. Brass and service ribbons covered his left jacket pocket, indicating he'd been in the armed forces for a very long time. Reflective aviator sunglasses hid his eyes. The shorter of the two men wore the same sunglasses, but his chest contained very few service ribbons and no brass.

She carefully walked down the stairs, her legs still trembling from the near-death experience and the booze.

Finally she stood on the tarmac, barely able to stop herself from kneeling and kissing the ground.

"Ellen?" asked the older officer with all the ribbons and colorful accoutrements decorating his chest, his thin lips forming a wide smile.

Peering at his shoulders, she saw two silver stars on each side. The guy was a general. Her eyes flitted to the younger of the two officers to see a single bar on each of his bony shoulders. She knew shit about military ranks but the young one had to be the junior officer. Probably the big man's aide or something.

"Uh, yeah. I'm Ellen McKee." Her eyes narrowed. *How does this man know my name?* "Who are you?"

The general removed his sunglasses, revealing warm brown eyes, the flesh beside them crinkled due to his wide grin. "It's me." He must have seen the lack of comprehension in her eyes because he chuckled and stepped forward to wrap her in his arms, hugging her to him. "Ed Dugan."

Ellen was stunned. *Ed?* She hadn't seen or heard from him in almost thirty years.

After *the event* in '55 when she was taken to Groom Air Force Base, she was accompanied—there's that word again—by Lieutenant Edward Dugan, a pimply-faced kid who claimed to be an officer. She'd only been nine years old at the time, but even then, Ed hadn't looked too much older than her.

Back then he'd been a jumpy, nervous, junior officer around her and the others. The others being Milt Swag and Ben Kwong who, so she was told later, had been with her at *the event*. The three had been at the epicenter of a blast by an atomic bomb that flattened Survivor Town and demonstrated the shocking destruction wrought by a weapon of mass destruction too terrible to be used.

During the cold war that followed, the United States and the U.S.S.R. were fearful of Mutual Assured Destruction, also known as MAD, because both sides recognized nuclear war was unwinnable.

After atomic bomb test Apple-2 in May of 1955, a few people would have disagreed since three seemingly normal children survived a holocaust of a destruction that should have vaporized them and no one knew why or how they'd survived or even why they were there. Not even she, Milt, or Ben had the answers to these questions. But Ellen badly wanted to know. That day had consumed most of her waking hours ever since and was the principal reason she drank. Unfortunately, their memories of what had happened to them had somehow been erased.

The three children had been reported missing by their parents two days before the bomb test, but all Ellen remembered of the time before she arrived at Groom Lake was playing with her dog in the front yard of her parents house. Milt and Ben had pretty much the same story.

The U.S. government had kept the incident secret since that day in 1955 and had sworn the children and their parents to secrecy by threatening them with life imprisonment for treason if they ever revealed their part in test Apple-2.

Now here was that same nervous lieutenant, now a general, welcoming her as if she were some long-lost friend. The mint of his mouthwash and the tang of his musky aftershave filled her nose. Finally he released her, with his hands still grasping her shoulders.

"How have you been?' he asked, his expression eager as a schoolboy.

"Uhhh...confused?"

General Dugan laughed. He dropped his hands to his sides. "Of course you are...I'm sorry..." He turned toward the pasty-faced, thin-as-a-toothpick, young officer who stood impassively watching them. "This is my aide, Lieutenant Mitchell, but ignore him. He's me thirty years ago."

The general laughed loudly at his joke, while Mitchell's brow wrinkled and his hazel eyes narrowed slightly. He then emitted a brief chuckle.

"Very good, sir," he said in a low monotone.

Dugan scoffed at his aide. "Of course it's good. I said it, Mitchell." He started to walk toward the waiting jeep. "Let's get out of here. We don't have much time.

"Sorry about the rough landing, Ellen; that seems to happen around her quite a bit. Folks get a little upset, but don't worry; it's perfectly normal."

Boy, has he changed, thought Ellen following after him. *He's been promoted to arrogant jerk.*

When she arrived at the jeep, Mitchell was holding the rear passenger door open for her. She climbed in and slid across the cloth seat. The interior of the jeep was much cooler than the oppressive desert heat outside. General Dugan climbed into the front passenger seat and his aide took the driver's seat.

Her eyes travelled to the mist-covered mountains in the distance across a barren, unforgiving landscape dotted with cacti and scrub brush. Waves of heat shimmered in the distance creating the illusion of water.

Memories of suddenly becoming aware of these surroundings flooded back, threatening to overwhelm her with the force of the memories of the fear, dread, and shock she'd felt on the day she found herself standing amongst the ruins of Survivor Town.

Looking ahead she could still see the ghost-like outline of the road that had led to the faux town thirty years ago.

"General, is this Survivor Town?" she asked.

General Dugan, who had his back to her as the jeep jerked into movement, the engine roaring in the confined space, turned to look at her, his eyes hard now. "Yes, at least where it used to be. We're headed for the spot where you, Milt, and Ben were found."

"Why?"

It was a simple question, one that had haunted her in many ways since that day, the day that changed the course of her life. Gazing into this now-old man's eyes, she knew his life had also been transformed by the experience. He had obviously had success in the military hierarchy, but something more was behind those eyes. Something he wasn't about to share with her or probably anyone. Much like her, Dugan was damaged goods.

When the jeep came to a stop, there were two jeeps already parked at a junction of three roads forming the spot known as ground zero. There was a group of men standing talking at the center of the junction. Some were in uniform, some in civilian garb.

Ellen swung open the door and climbed out, again struck by how hot it was. Mitchell was thoughtful enough to hand her a pair of sunglasses like those he and the general were wearing.

Her heart suddenly almost leapt from her chest when she spotted two familar faces amongst the knot of men. The faces were older, fuller to be sure, but unmistakable. Ben and Milt were here, too.

Racing across the road, she threw her arms around Ben and hugged him. With tears staining her cheeks, she released him, then did the same to Milt. They, too, were driven to tears by the sudden reunion. They had shared an experience like none other in history.

Ellen gathered herself and released Milt. They gazed at each other happily between a blur of tears, unable to speak.

"Ten minutes, sir," said Mitchell from where he stood to their right near the jeep that had brought Ellen to this spot.

Ellen stopped crying and turned to glare at Dugan. "What's really going on, General?"

Dugan avoided her stare. "Well, you see, we've never been certain how you three survived the blast and we thought if we brought you here again when we tested a new weapon system, we might learn your secret."

Ellen looked to the other two survivors. Both Ben's and Milt's eyes registered their surprise and confusion. She looked back at Dugan. "Do you mean you *hope* we'll survive?"

Dugan nodded. "Listen, I'm sorry about this, but surely you don't think we can just let it go and not try to determine why you all survived the blast in '55. We have to know how you did it."

36

"So you can build a newer, better defensive system, or maybe a weapon to better kill commies? Correct?" Ellen asked, her eyes narrowing. She had never trusted these bastards.

Dugan nodded.

Mitchell walked up to him carrying an attaché case. He laid it on the hood of one of the jeeps and opened it. Inside were three smooth gray stones, scarred with markings etched into the surface of the stones.

"We still have these."

She watched his Adam's apple bob as he swallowed. "We found you three holding them in your hands after we discovered you in this exact spot. We've run every test on them we know and they came back exactly as what they appear: inert rock. Unremarkable in every way."

Ellen stared at the stones resting in cloth pockets in the case and something came over her. Fog crept in from the sides of her eyes, blurring first her vision, then clouding her mind. The oppressive heat, the desert, the men, the rush of the steady breeze blowing grains of fine sand across her cheeks, her friends—everything and everyone disappeared in the fog.

***

May 8, 2015
Apartment 16D - Bayview Apartments - Boston, Massachusetts

The television's volume was set low while Ellen worked on her latest knitting project.

Sandra Lebowski and her husband Adam in apartment 8A were having their first child soon and she wanted to finish the knitted sleeper before the baby arrived. Ellen liked Sandy and Adam. They were a nice couple.

Her eyes drifted up to the television screen while her fingers worked the knitting needles. Castle had just described one of his preposterous theories of the crime. She chuckled to herself. The guy was *so* handsome, and *so* dumb.

The intercom buzzer sounded, interrupting her thoughts. Sighing, she stood and ambled to the intercom, set in the wall next to the hallway door. Pressing the red button, she activated the speaker. "Hello?" She released the button so whoever was at the other end could speak.

"It's Agent Wilson of the NSA, ma'am. We're here to pick you up for your flight."

Ellen rolled her eyes, then pressed the button again. "Okay. I'll be down in ten minutes." Releasing the button, she ambled to the bedroom to collect her small overnight bag. She wasn't about to be unprepared this time.

Of course, it helped this time that the general had called her in advance, telling her they were testing a particle beam weapon. From his description, the weapon would make for one hell of a big punch. He said it might actually penetrate the shield. Good for the military, bad for them.

Time was growing short.

The alien attack force had entered the solar system. Ellen, Milt, and Ben had agreed to make the ultimate sacrifice if it would save the human race from annihilation.

But like much of the human race, they were survivors.

She hadn't had a drink of alcohol since that day in 1985—she didn't want her mind clouded by anything she could control ever again—after the space defense system weapons test, or as the press called it, Star Wars, named after the energy weapons depicted in the popular science fiction movie series.

Every few years the military took her and the others to the weapons testing ground to test their latest weapon of mass destruction, hoping they'd learn the truth behind the stones. And they hoped to discover why she, Ben, and Milt were able to survive the destruction of the newest model of death ray, or whatever, created by the next generation of mad scientists. The government was becoming increasingly desperate due to the looming threat to the planet.

She turned off the television and collected her pre-packed suitcase, rolling it across her carpeted floor on its wheels to the front closet, where she retrieved her thin nylon windbreaker and slipped on her open-toed leather sandals.

Taking one last look around her one bedroom apartment, she doubted she'd see her home again. If this test failed, she was convinced the government would dissect her and the others. They needed the secret of their survival, even if it meant cutting them open to get it.

She smirked as she opened the door and walked into the hall. The problem was, she wanted answers too. Even if she had to die to get them.

She could refuse to go, but she knew she had no choice; and General Mitchell hated to be kept waiting.

The door closed behind her with a dull *thump*.

Ghosts and crime have been fodder for some legendary stories. This is another in the Amanda Dark, Paranormal Investigator series where Amanda must confront dark family secrets with extreme personal stakes.

Moonrise Diner

THE CUSHIONS OF PHILLIP SWANN'S BLACK LEATHER EXECUTIVE CHAIR sighed breaking the silence of the teak wood paneled office as he sank into the chair. Amanda Dark sat in a horseshoe shaped chair studying him from the other side of his massive glass-topped desk. His intense blue eyes were fixed on the letter he'd unfolded seconds ago after extracting it from the yellowing envelope Amanda handed him when she sat down.

His jet-black curly hair, cut short as usual, appealed to her more every day they spent together. Her heart beat a little faster each time they met. If only he shared her deeper feelings.

The law offices of Smythe, Wellington, Goldberg, and Thompson smelled of wood polish, which wasn't surprising since the Boston law firm had never removed the original teak paneling from the walls since it the firm first opened in 1902. Such expensive wood required constant care to maintain its gleaming, pristine appearance.

Amanda imagined such attention to detail gave the firm's wealthy clients considerable confidence in the expertise of the firms seventy-five lawyers. Amanda eyed Phillip's square jaw, dimpled smile, and broad shoulders causing her heart to flutter.

41

I certainly have confidence in the man I've loved since we met on Hook Island.

Their first meeting had been eventful and dangerous so it wasn't a stretch to remember those events. Phillip invited her to Hook Island hoping she'd use her gift to help the ghost of the notorious pirate, Captain Henry Swann, his ancestor, to cross over to his final destination in order to free the pirate captain from his wanderings between this world and the next. And to ask Phillip's ancestor the location of a map so he could find Captain Swann's buried treasure reported to be worth a fortune.

Since then Phillip, as an estate attorney, had teamed up with her, in her role as a paranormal investigator, to help a number of tortured souls to cross over. The jobs had been rewarding and lucrative for them both. Wealthy clients paid considerable sums for their services.

Phillip finished reading the three-page letter then set it carefully on his desk. The document was quite old since it dated back to the nineteen fifties. She knew this because it originated in her late father's files.

Amanda found the envelope in a file folder stuffed with power company bills dated in the early fifties she'd been about to throw away. She didn't open the envelope addressed to her father because the return address was for her Uncle Gib's place in Arizona.

Uncle Gib, her father's older brother, had sexually abused her when she was twelve so anything he touched repulsed her. Her first thought was to burn the envelope to a pile of ash, to join her uncle who no doubt burned in hell, but something deep within her told her not to destroy this envelope. These feelings were something more than mere emotions it was important she listen to the spiritual voices calling to her.

The postmark showed the letter was mailed from Moonrise Arizona. The date stamp in the postmark intrigued her the most because it was the day her uncle murdered his first wife, Lucy. Or at least the day he *allegedly* stabbed her to death.

Her uncle had been acquitted of the murder, but had lived under a cloud of suspicion for the rest of his life. Family legend said Gib remarried, his second wife also named Luci (the only difference being her name ended in an i instead of a y), like his first wife, worked as a waitress with him at the Moonrise Diner. There could have been physical differences as well, but Amanda never met either of them so she had no idea what they looked like.

As far as she knew no one in the family had ever met Luci the second even after Gib died. Frankly Amanda thought there never was a second wife.

Amanda searched the on-line newspaper archives after she found the envelope and discovered coverage of Gib's trial. There was no mention in any of the news articles referring to a letter mailed to her father on the day of Gib's arrest. And there was no mention of her father testifying at her uncle's trial.

Her father told her he turned his back on his brother after his arrest, until after she was born when they reconciled. Her father never explained how they buried the figurative hatchet to settle their differences.

At the time Uncle Gib abused her she feared if she told her father it would create another split between the two brothers so she remained silent. Fortunately the abuse only happened once then Gib left Boston for the last time. When Amanda was thirteen Gibb ended his own life.

She'd blocked his name from her mind for the past fourteen years until she found the envelope.

Phillip, his eyes on the desk, his head forward, didn't say anything for several minutes. The suspense formed a knot of tension in Amanda's stomach and she grew increasingly restless as each second passed passing the time by shifting her bottom on the leather chair repeatedly as if she were unable to get comfortable. Finally, she couldn't contain herself any further. "Phillip, for goodness sake, what does it say?"

Phillip looked up from the desk, his eyes free of emotion, to lock eyes with her. One eyebrow arched on his tanned forehead. "Your uncle wasn't who he said he was."

Her heart skipped a beat. *Breath, girl....*"What do you mean?"

Phillip sat back and sighed. "He claims he was an undercover operative for the Arizona State Police. He says someone killed his wife to send him a message."

"Does he say who?" Now she was extremely interested. This had quickly become a mystery. She loved a mystery.

Phillip gazed at her a pained expression on his face. "Something about inappropriate advances on a woman." He looked away avoiding her stare.

Amanda's guts twisted pushing the acid taste of bile into the back of her throat. She thought she might vomit any second. She shuddered as the awful memory swept over her of her uncle's hands groping her. Memories of the stale liquor on his breath, mingling with the smell of salty sweat, and the spent cooking grease leaching from his pores paralyzed her.

"Does he know who killed his wife?" she whispered in a trembling voice. Calling on inner reserves she pushed through the decades of pain and humiliation. Phillip shook his head.

44

Her Uncle Gib was a creepy, lying, sack of...but he was her beloved father's brother whose wife had apparently been murdered by persons unknown. And who knew now if his death was a suicide? Everything about the letter cast uncertainty on her uncle's life requiring closer scrutiny. In respect for her dad's love for his brother she would solve this mystery, given her history with her uncle she just didn't want to.

"I'll call the Arizona State Police then," she decided. "They'll look into the murder." Phillip shook his head again the difference this time being his eyes drooped at the corners.

A sudden burst of anger welled up from deep within Amanda's belly. *I don't need his pity.*

"Did I say something wrong?" asked Phillip, his eyes wide with concern.

"Why do you ask?"

Phillip's expression relaxed. "Ummm, I know this is a stressful situation, Amanda, and I'm sorry, I truly am." A gentle smile passed over his handsome features.

When she brought him the envelope she told him how she didn't like her uncle and that he was estranged from the family, but didn't share the details of the sexual abuse. But her would-be boyfriend was a smart man; he knew something was very wrong even if he didn't know the details. "But the Arizona State cops are unlikely to take any interest in reopening the case. They seemed convinced your uncle committed the crime"

Amanda picked up the glass of water Phillip poured for her when she first arrived and took a sip of the cool water as the tension in her body eased. "Why not? I'm sure they want to catch the real murderer."

45

Phillip nodded. "Of course, but the case was likely closed after your uncle's trial because they probably still think he's guilty, or got off on some technically, or he had a clever lawyer." His mouth formed a sly smile. "They don't much care for the practioners of my profession. And if you tell them you're a paranormal investigator they'll laughed us both out of the police station."

Amanda's cheeks grew warm. "What's wrong with my job?"

Phillip arched one eyebrow. "Now, Amanda, I don't mean to offend you, I know from personal experience you have a special gift, but police officers are born skeptics. They'll never take you seriously." He sighed then lifted his coffee mug to his lips and took a sip. After swallowing he added, "I think the better approach is to search the scene of the crime for ourselves. Maybe we'll find something, or someone that'll help us uncover the truth. Something the cops overlooked all those years ago."

The anger disappeared as Amanda considered his words. He was right. They both knew the *something* or *someone* Phillip referred to involved ghosts and the paranormal.

"OK," she said, "the place to start is the town of Moonrise, Arizona. That's where Gib had his diner—his wife, Lucy, died in the diner..." Her brow wrinkled. "And I seem to recall dad telling me Gib committed suicide in the diner."

Her well tuned sixth sense for the supernatural told her they would find a horrible truth at the Moonrise Diner, a frightening truth that made her blood run cold.

***

The two lanes of cracked asphalt making up the main street of Moonrise Arizona were off the state highway on an old highway bypass carved from the dry, desolate landscape surrounding the abandoned mining town.

46

According to the GPS navigator the by pass ended five miles north of the town.

Amanda spent the several hours driving to Moonrise from the Phoenix airport on her iPad reviewing her uncle's trial transcript Phillip had managed to obtain for her. She was surprised the file even existed any more, but was please it was found in the Arizona State Government Library.

The transcript did yield some interesting facts. In 1972 Uncle Gib testified he and Lucy had a fierce argument the night Lucy was killed after which he went to a nearby bar to cool off ending up going on a drinking binge. There were a plethora of names related to the case—small time gangsters mostly, with colorful names like; Pete "Split Nose" Rostovitch, Jimmy "Beer Belly" Lucia, Al "Stinky" Garbone, and "Maximum Guts" Max Schiller.

Uncle Gib claimed one of these gangsters killed his wife, but his reasons for thinking this were absent from the record. The cops or the district attorney obviously didn't believe his allegations, or they didn't want to believe him.

She put her iPad away in her handbag as Phillip stopped their rented Jeep in front of the Moonrise Hotel. Amanda expected to see a hitching post for horses and cowboys with ten-gallon hats and leather gun belts strapped to their hips standing on the porch.

Instead a gray haired man sat in a rocking chair reading a newspaper on the porch to one side of the twin doors of the hotel entrance. The doors had glass windows built into the wood frame allowing her to see the lobby and the front desk. A gray haired woman stood behind the desk her eyes focused on something in front of her.

Phillip shut off the engine then swung the drivers door open as the rumble of the engine died away replaced by the soft whisper of the desert wind.

The oppressive heat struck her in the face as soon as she swung the door open. Her skin immediately became damp with sweat as she stepped into the thick, hot, air.

Phillip retrieved their suitcases from the back of the jeep then joined her walking up the three steps to the wide gray wood porch, the boards creaking underfoot.

The man in the rocker dropped his newspaper and his coffee colored eyes narrowed. "Heya, you folks lookin' for a room?" His voice had a scratchy quality like an old phonograph record.

"Yes," said Amanda with a nice-to-meet-you smile on her lips. "We're in town on holiday."

The man chuckled gruffly letting the newspaper fall into his lap. "Holiday? In Moonrise? That's a good one, young lady." He arched one white eyebrow. "No one holidays in this town. It's nearly dead. Me and the wife are the last of the few who stayed after the silver mine closed."

"When was that?" asked Phillip.

The old man snorted. "Back in '99. The mining company ran out of money...they left town along with most of the folks 'round here." He peered into the distance ignoring them. "We had a pretty young school marm, a church, General Store and even one of them fancy haberdasheries.... those were the days..." He scowled then abruptly raised the newspaper creating a wall of newsprint between them. "Never been the same since," he muttered.

Amanda shook her head then caught herself when she spotted the date at the top of the paper in the old man's hands. November twenty-first, nineteen ten.

That can't be right. Has to be a misprint.

Phillip opened one of the twin glass and wood doors and ushered her inside. Once in the hotel lobby the smell of dust and sand disappeared replaced by the scent of jasmine and though the air was warm it was cooler so than outside. The reception desk, made of weathered wood planks, sat to the left of a wide sweeping staircase, reminiscent of Gone With the Wind, which rose from the flowered carpeted lobby to disappear to the floors above.

A woman behind the desk cast her dispassionate gaze over them. The collar of her old fashioned long sleeved dress covered her long, narrow neck to just under her angular chin. Her hollow, sunken eyes were the color of obsidian and her complexion reminded Amanda of white glue. *Maybe she's ill...*

"Hello," she said in a rasping voice. "May I help you?"

"Yes, ma'am," said Phillip his tone musical and friendly. Overly friendly, it sounded false to Amanda and probably everyone else. She cringed inside. Regardless he continued. "We need two rooms, please."

The old woman smirked then flopped open a register sending a puff of dust into air.

Amanda waved away the dust blinking her eyes to clear them. "Two rooms?" she whispered to Phillip. "Why don't we share one? It'd be cheaper."

He turned his head slightly to look at her. "Best to have separate rooms." He grinned. "I might not be able to control myself."

Amanda offered a weak grin. *I only wish.* She immediately scolded herself. *I'm acting like a lovesick schoolgirl; I'm a grown woman.*

"How long have you been here?" Amanda asked the woman.

"All my life, Miss."

"Sorry, I meant how long has the hotel been here?"

"Longer than I have."

Amanda studied the woman looking for signs she was joking, but she appeared to be serious so Amanda shifted her gaze to look at Phillip. He offered her a humorless smile but didn't say anything.

After Phillip signed the register for them both the old woman placed two old-fashioned brass keys with yellowing paper tags attached to the ends. Her eyes dropped to peer at the two names Phillip had recorded in the ledger.

"Mr. Swann, I gave you room 212," her eyes shifted to Amanda, "room 312 for you, Miss Dark." The woman's tone was clipped and registered her disapproval of Amanda.

I guess she doesn't like questions.

"I'll carry your bag to your room," offered Phillip.

"No, thank you, *Mr.* Swann, I carry my own weight." Amanda snatched her room key off the desk then, after grabbing her bag by the handle, hurried up the curved carpeted staircase headed for the rooms on the upper floors.

"I'll meet you here in the lobby in half an hour," Phillip called after her.

"OK." Without looking back she hurried up the creaking stairs. She hoped they had Wi-Fi. The man and woman running the hotel seemed strangely out of place, though they claimed to have been living in Moonrise all their lives. She needed to conduct some research about the town and its remaining inhabitants.

***

The first thing she noticed upon entering the room was the smell. It reeked of mothballs and cigarette smoke.

There was old-fashioned gas lamp on an end table next to an antique burnished brass bed frame containing a too soft mattress that sagged badly under the weight of her suitcase, which wasn't much since she'd packed light.

After tossing her suitcase on the bed she set up her laptop on the cheap pine table set under the window over looking the street in front of the hotel.

Moving the matching chair away from the desk she sat down and flipped the laptop open. After booting it up she saw there was no Wi-Fi connection.

Disappointed she next opened the folder with the pictures she'd downloaded of her uncle's diner, from the family electronic archive her sister set up years before, then clicked through them one by one. As she studied the photos her mouth became dry and a lump of emotion grew in her throat as memories, both good and bad, washed over her.

She stopped clicking the cursor now hovering over an image of Uncle Gib's diner back in the days he and Lucy owned it wondering if she'd overcome her fears and dread to be able to go inside. But she knew she had to, it was the only way she'd discover the truth.

Swiping the screen with her finger the image of the pristine diner was replaced by a picture of the diner that had become severely dilapidated in the intervening decades, since it had been abandoned after her uncle's death.

Somehow Amanda knew they'd discover the ghost of Lucy Dark haunting the old diner. When Lucy died her killer was never brought to justice for her murder.

In Amanda's experience this created the perfect paranormal recipe for spirits of the dead to be unable to cross over.

Searching out Lucy's ghost seemed the only way to gain the information she and Phillip would need, and perhaps to bring a killer to justice and put an end to Lucy's wanderings.

The diner was now a severely neglected building, the wind and blowing sand having peeled most of the paint off the sign and the gray, weathered wood siding. There was a rusting nineteen forties pick up truck, the tires missing, sitting on blocks under all four wheels, beside the crumbling restaurant.

She traced the image of the diner on the screen with her index finger and sighed. At times like this she wished the man who once was her favorite uncle, something until this moment she had forced herself to forget, had stayed as she remembered him...before...a sob escaped her lips then she began to weep uncontrollably.

***

Phillip stood in the lobby facing the street watching two tumbleweeds being pushed along by the constant desert wind. There were no signs of the old man or woman he was alone. Dressed in tanned walking shorts, a navy blue golf shirt, and white Nikes, he had a pair of sunglasses raised high on his forehead.

"Hey, Amanda, ready to go?"

"Hi, Phillip," Amanda said, stepping off the last step of the staircase onto the worn oriental carpet.

Having changed into her exploration garb she spun around showing off her white walking shorts, mustard yellow blouse and white open toed sandals. "What do you think?"

Her unpleasant mood when she last saw Phillip had disappeared. A good cry so often cleared out the cobwebs in her head. She hated being used it ruined her day.

It wasn't his fault her uncle molested her, Phillip had treated her like a princess, he deserved better treatment.

Phillip turned toward her smiling like the Cheshire cat. What was he up to now?

"You look good enough to take out on the town." He cocked one eyebrow. "Especially in this town."

He was joking of course, but she didn't really care where they went provided they did it together. "Oh, Mr. Swann, you say the naughtiest things."

He chuckled. "OK, Ms. Dark, let's go to the old diner and look for some clues. What do you say?"

She swallowed a sudden lump fear in the back of her throat. "Sounds like a plan." She walked to stand beside him as he offered the crook of his arm. Grinning at him she ran one hand around his offered arm.

***

Amanda played the stream of white light emitted by the heavy-duty flashlight gripped in her sweaty, pale hand over the inky dark interior of the deserted roadside diner. Her heartbeat hard in her chest, her dry mouth had a slightly metallic taste. Her tongue flicked over her lips.

She wondered where the ghost was hiding. It could be anywhere, in the walls, in the floor, in the kitchen cooking eggs. She swallowed a chuckle. This was of course impossible. The power and water had been shut off after her uncle died.

It had taken an hour to walk to the diner at the edge of town near the highway. Her feet hurt and she was thirstier than she had ever been in her life, but Phillip seemed as fresh as when they set off. He wanted to continue so she reluctantly agreed.

Why couldn't they have brought the car?

When they arrived outside the diner the sun had dropped to near the horizon. It would be dark in an hour. The doors and windows of the diner were boarded up, but together they managed to pry ones off the front door to get inside. Not that it was all that difficult since the wooden boards and the wood door were dry and badly rotted by the desert conditions over the past two decades of neglect. Once inside they had to use flashlights in order to see.

"We don't get a lot of customers these days," said woman's voice coming from the their right.

A six-foot section of counter—a section of which appeared to be have crumbled away due to rot—and six rusted round steel stools in front were all that remained of the original lunch counter. The fabric of the booths seats beside the boarded up windows across were dusty and ripped, the stuffing hanging out in great clumps, as if torn apart by wild animals.

The voice continued, "Not since they built the bypass."

"The bypass was built in 1962," whispered Phillip in Amanda's ear.

Amanda realized the voice must belong to Gib's first wife.

"Uhhh, Lucy? Is that you?" Swinging her flashlight beam she discovered a woman standing behind the counter, a waitress dressed in a pink uniform skirt and matching blouse. Her fiery red curls were partially covered a little white trimmed pink hat, in one hand she held a green and white order pad, in the other hand a glass carafe filled with black coffee. Steam actually rose from inside the carafe.

The waitress — obviously a ghost as evidenced by her ivory, pale complexion and unblinking stare—wore a sardonic smile on her bloodless lips and her pale green eyes reflecting curiosity.

"Yes, are you two cops or sumthin'?" Lucy's ghost didn't wait for a response instead she grunted then took a step farther down the dusty counter away from them. She poured a measure of coffee into a dusty white china mug on the counter.

Amanda assumed Lucy could see whoever was seated at the counter but she couldn't. It was an odd restriction of her gift, something she had experience a few times before, certain ghosts left behind echoes of the host after the spirit itself crossed over. It happened maybe one in a half a million times, so while it wasn't that common she had seen it before.

Lucy's ghost recognized these echoes and thought they were as *real* as herself. Ghosts were unable to discern echoes from other ghosts. This particular echo must have been a customer of the diner.

"Why don't you cops move along and stop bothering old Barney and I. " 'Aint that right, Barney?" Lucy winked at the empty stool in front of the counter.

"Uhhh, Lucy—" began Amanda.

Lucy's ghost set the carafe on the counter and turned to silence Amanda with a glare and Phillip who both had their flashlights trained on her. "Do I know you people?" Amanda shook her head. "Then how do you know my name?"

Amanda hesitated. It was a good question and one that deserved a response. "Well, you see I'm Gib Darks' niece—"

Lucy's features were suddenly split by a wide grin and she rushed to stand in front of Amanda the ghostly figure now sparkling under the light from the two flashlights.

"You're, Mandy?" Lucy spoke excitedly. "Well, why didn't you say so when you came in?" Lucy turned to look at the pass bar beyond which was the kitchen. "Hey, Gib, Mandy's here!"

Amanda froze, her hands trembled causing the flashlight beam to shake, and her heart beat rapidly in her chest. The swinging door separating the counter from the kitchen hung at an angle on one hinge. He'd have to pass through the wall...

A sudden wave of dizziness gripped her. Reaching out to grip the edge of the counter in order to steady herself made the beam of light to wave about wildly. Phillip's flashlight also swung about crazily so she knew he was experiencing the same thing as her.

The feeling quickly passed but from the corner of one eye Amanda saw the diner had started to physically change. Amanda's heart skipped a beat. The diner was transforming, some how reverting to a past time when the diner was new.

"Impossible," she whispered under her breath.

The weathered gray wall, the paint peeling from the crumbling plaster farthest away, straightened and became smooth then changed from gray to a mint green. Next the section of the counter that had been missing reappeared as if from nothing.

The white-gray speckled linoleum tiles on the floor looked freshly waxed. The light fixtures lining the ceiling changed from broken and rusted to gleaming stainless steel with glowing blubs. The light fixtures now too looked to be newly installed.

As the wave touched the stools in front of the counter they began to change from rusting relics to shiny new under the glow of the lights. Even the seat fabric of the booths against the windows and the stools, now a shiny aquamarine color, appeared to be brand new with not one tear or mark.

Like a fast moving tsunami the changes spread across the diner racing toward them unrelenting and undulating as if alive. As the wave of change was about to engulf them Amanda closed her eyes and held her breath.

Nothing happened for several seconds, but she was too afraid to move.

"Hey, Mandy, what's wrong?" *Uncle Gib?*

The soft burr of an air conditioner motor sent a gentle breeze of cold air over her. When they first walked in the musty collapsing diner had been too warm and too humid. After releasing the air from her lungs she sucked in a breath of the cool air. It felt so good.

Opening one eye she saw a much younger version than she remembered of her Uncle Gib coming toward her through the now brand new swinging door from the kitchen. With his square jaw and dark wavy hair he looked as real and solid as if he were still alive. The man was grinning.

Sucking in another breath she closed her eyes again as she struggled to steady her nerves. The transformation of an environment had never happened during a paranormal investigation, it was too incredible, too unbelievable to be real, but it was real.

How is this possible?

She opened both eyes to find herself looking into the coal black pupils of the man who molested her. This man was her Uncle Gib.

***

Seated at the lunch counter, her bottom resting on the soft cushion, Amanda sipped from the clean glass of water held in her trembling fingers. Phillip sat on the stool beside her sipping water from an identical glass filled with clear water. Her scream of shock still seemed to echo off the restaurants' walls.

Lucy and Gib stood leaning back against the waist high fridges beneath the service counter built into the wall behind them. To their right, in the wall, was an opening with the stainless steel pass bar where prepared food was placed awaiting pick up by a waitress. Three heat lamps ran along the top edge of the opening shining down on the pass bar to keep the orders warm until they were picked up.

As if Amanda's aunt and uncle weren't in the room, Phillip asked her to explain the transformation of the diner's interior, but she was unable to offer any explanation since she'd never seen this happen before. It surprised her he was able to see it happen too. This was way beyond her experience or expertise and, she was afraid to admit, it frightened her.

The diner now looked brand new as if they had been transported to 1957 no longer in 2014. Time travel was impossible so she concluded this was some sort of paranormal event unlike anything she'd ever witnessed.

"Ummm," she began her voice tentative, "Uncle Gib did you build the diner?"

Uncle Gib focused his black eyes on her and nodded. "Yes, me and Lucy did all the work ourselves with our own two hands." His eyes were humorless and his tanned forehead was marred by a frown.

After the diner was regenerated (Amanda decided the word regenerated best described what they'd witnessed) Gib and Lucy became fully human again, but in their younger bodies. They looked as real and alive as Amanda and Phillip; even their cheeks were flushed as if they had blood in their veins.

Amanda's well-tuned sense for all things paranormal told
her when they left the diner it would revert to its former dilapidated
condition. She wished she had an explanation for all this that made
some sense.

My gift really messes with my head some days.

Fortunately she'd seen enough weird things on this job that
one more strange unexpected happening eventually seemed actually
normal on some level.

"I'm so sorry, Uncle Gibb," she said finally able to look her
uncle in the eyes.

Gib shrugged but both he and Lucy didn't look happy. "You
scared away all our customers," blurted Lucy. "We have bills to pay
ya know."

Gib shifted his gaze to his wife and placed one hand on her
shoulder. "Take it easy, honey. Mandy's always been high strung."

As if struck by a bolt from a blue sky an idea suddenly struck
Amanda. "If this is the fifties then I haven't been born yet. How
would you know what I'm like?"

Gib winced. Grinning sheepishly he said, "I don't know,
Mandy. I have access to all of the memories from my corporeal
existence. Even..." his voice trailed off as his cheeks flushed
crimson.

A familar tingle of anger swelled in Amanda's belly but she
forced it down. Anger would only lead to more pain, now that she
had him in front of her she might finally get the answers she'd been
seeking all her life. "Yes, of course...I'm curious about your death
and Lucy's—" She stopped uncertain if she should break the news of
Lucy's murder to the victim.

Lucy slammed a fist into Gib's shoulder causing him to wince
in pain. "How does she know about that?" Gibb shrugged.

I guess she knows already. "It's OK, Lucy," Amanda said, "I found an envelope containing a letter Gib wrote in my father's files after he died." She eyed her uncle who appeared very much alive. Death seemed a debatable concept right now so she decided not to tell Lucy about Gib's suicide. She sensed Lucy didn't know everything about her husband, which actually made sense since she died before Gib crawled into a whiskey bottle, and before he molested Amanda.

"Anyway, regardless of our present circumstance I know, Lucy, you were murdered based on the contents of Uncle Gib's letter. He claims he was an undercover operative for the Arizona State Police and someone was sending him a message by killing you."

Gib nodded his head dropping to his chest. "She's right." His voice was barely audible.

Lucy's pale features twisted in anger as she raised her fist and hit him in the shoulder again this time harder than before. "You son of a...you used me...Milt killed me didn't he?" Gib groaned and wrapped his injured arm with his left hand. "Didn't he!" Lucy arms were at her sides with her hands curled into fists.

Gib nodded but remained silent.

"Uhhh, who's, Milt?' asked Amanda. She thought about asking about the gangsters mentioned in the trial transcript but she wanted to hear this first.

Lucy looked at her. "Milt was his partner on the police force. I've never met anyone so jealous as that pig." She shuddered. "An awful man, crude, drank too much...he craved violence ya know?"

"Was this before or after you started the diner?' asked Phillip.

Lucy stepped away from her cowed husband crossing her arms over her chest. "Not that it matters now, but Gib started this diner to escape his old job as a cop."

She shifted her eyes to glare at Gib who avoided her. "*We* were tired of the danger, the late nights, no days off, his crazy partner...all of it. Frankly, if Gib didn't leave the state police we were through."

"Where can we find this Milt?" asked Phillip.

Gib looked at Amanda through bloodshot eyes. "Milton Spender lives in a nursing home in Phoenix." Her uncle looked so sad she couldn't help up feel sorry for him. Before she dealt with the problem with Lucy she needed to air some family laundry.

"Uncle Gib..." she began the old dark fear rising from within her closed her throat. Pushing her fear aside she continued. "Uncle Gib, why did you molest me?"

He stuffed his hands in the pockets of his white cook pants while avoiding her eyes. "I'm so sorry, Mandy. I was drunk. I had a problem." He hesitated. "I told your father what happened promising never to return to Boston." He locked eyes with her, his filled with tears. "I know it's not an acceptable excuse but please, please forgive me. I've loved you like the daughter I never had since I first saw you at the hospital when you were born."

His eyes pleaded with her for forgiveness. Slowly the fear that had consumed her life, the shame that permeated her soul since she was twelve years old began to recede. After more than two decades a terrible burden lifted from her shoulders.

She looked at Phillip hoping he might help her to decide, but since he didn't know how badly her uncle hurt her until this moment he couldn't really help. He hadn't lived this terrible secret. He gazed at her with sad eyes, a weak smile on his lips. While she sensed Phillip's sympathy only she could decide.

"Alright, Uncle Gib..." Her words caught in her throat and a shiver ran down her spine, but she pushed herself through the fear.

"I'll...forgive you..."

A sudden feeling of pure joy shot from her toes to her head. Her words had set her free from of the past. Her paranormal senses tingled signaling she had done the correct thing by forgiving someone who so impacted her life.

Gib buried his head in his hands and began to sob while Lucy stroked his back. She looked at Amanda. "Thank you," she said softly.

Turning away Phillip wrapped her in his arms, pulled her to him and stroked her shoulder. She rested her head against his chest feeling the steady beating of his heart against her.

"We have to visit this, Milton Spender," she said. "Lucy needs our help."

Phillip chuckled lightly. "That's my girl always thinking of others." He released her and grasped her shoulders with both hands gazing into her eyes. "How're you doing?"

"I've never felt better in my life," she said and meant it.

***

Upon driving through the iron gates of the retirement community where Milton Spender lived, Amanda saw nothing like the retirement homes she'd seen before, or even imagined a retirement community could be. The sprawling perfectly manicured facilities had to be exclusive to the very, very rich. No one of middle-class means could afford such a place so how a retired cop would be living in such a community?

Designed around a massive park with sprawling flower beds of roses, gardenias, and mature Rhododendrons covered with red, white and yellow flowers bordered tennis courts, an Olympic sized pool, and even a full eighteen hole golf course.

The magnificent grounds reminded Amanda more of a five star resort than a place where old folks went to die.

Amanda forgot to ask Uncle Gib about the gangsters, but decided it was too thin a line to follow since Lucy and Gib seemed adamant Milt Spender was the killer. Still something niggled at the back of her mind telling her something wasn't right, but she couldn't put a finger on what was bothering her.

After parking under the breezeway covering the entrance, Amanda with Phillip by her side entered the lobby through the twin glass doors after a female valet took the keys for their rental car saying she would park it for them.

The lobby smelled of lemon floor polish with gleaming marble tiles covering the floor finally ending at the massive reception desk. Behind the desk sat a man with slicked back black haircut close to his large head, wearing a white nurses uniform. As they approached the desk Amanda spotted a nametag over his left breast pocket that read, C. Reddick.

Forcing her best glad-to-meet-you smile on her lips as they arrived at the desk she said, "Hello. We're looking for Milton Spender."

Reddick, whose black eyes were focused on a document on the desk, looked up at them. "Milt? Why would you want ta see that old son of a bitch?"

Startled for a few seconds that Reddick would speak of a resident this way Amanda waited several seconds before speaking. "Uhhh, well, we have an old friend who knows Milt and wants us to check in on him." Her mouth formed a weak smile. "To see if he's okay."

Reddick snorted derisively and rose from the chair he'd been sitting in. "It's your funeral, lady."

He walked to stand in front of a bulletin board affixed to the wall behind him. After scanning a document pegged to the board he said, "Milt should be in the music appreciation class, that is if he felt like it today." He grunted. "Every days an adventure with Milt."

Shaking his head he walked back to sit in the chair. "Got ID?"

Phillip pulled out his wallet while Amanda opened her purse and extracted her driver's license from a pocket inside. After Reddick looked over their identification he asked them to sign their names in a visitors register.

"Folks from Boston come all the way to Phoenix to see a bastard like Milt Spender..." He snorted again. "Makes no difference to me, but you've come a long way for nuthin'." He handed them each a fire engine red plasticized visitors pass with a clip to attached to their breast pockets instructing them to display them at all times while on the premises.

"Thank you, Mr. Reddick. Which way to the class?"

Reddick pointed to the wide hallway left of the desk filled with older men and women shuffling along aided by walkers, some in wheel chairs, others in track suits walking briskly along their sport shoes squeaking on the tiled floor. To a person they all appeared happy and content. "Follow the yellow line on the wall to G Wing, Room 128A."

Amanda turned to face Phillip. Lowering her voice so Reddick couldn't hear them she said, "Why don't you find a place for a coffee? I want to speak with Mr. Spender by myself." Phillip opened his mouth to speak until she placed one finger over his lips. "No questions, please. I need to do this alone."

Phillip nodded but his eyes told her he wasn't happy about her decision.

Nevertheless he disappeared in the opposite direction after asking passing nurse directions for the cafeteria.

Amanda watched him go her stomach jumping to its own beat since her nerves were on edge. This case had given her a nervous stomach. She hadn't been sleeping well since starting the trek to Arizona, and meeting her uncle and aunt's younger ghosts hadn't helped her condition. True, a major emotional weight had been lifted from her after she forgave Gib, but she had the sinking feeling this visit to Milt wasn't going to end well.

She made her way along the maze of hallways following the yellow line painted on wall until she found G Wing. A sign with arrows under the big letter G showed room 128A was to the left.

Taking in a deep breath she headed down the hallway letting the air escape her lungs and taking another deep breath as she walked. She passed a number of the white haired residents, all of who nodded as they offered her close-mouthed smiles. With all the smiling Amanda began to wonder of this was the Stepford senior's home and all these people were duplicates created by computers and microchips.

The nurses she passed on the other hand didn't even look in her direction causing her to wonder about the effectiveness of the security system. In Amanda's line of work you tend to look at the details of a place when entering unknown territory. Often the minutiae of a place told you more than the people or the larger, more elaborate details.

Staff who ignored the most basic security protocol showed they couldn't care less about the place where they worked and its residents, or the security personnel were incompetent, lazy, or both.

Sure enough a portly man appeared from around a corner coming in her direction wearing a white shirt with shoulder patches reading *Security*, and black slacks. His blond hair was cut to half an inch from his round head. He rode a Segway. Dark sunglasses hid his eyes and the belt around his waist was heavy with all sorts of rattling tools, and numerous leather pouches.

As he rolled to a stop beside her he gazed at her. The portable radio on his belt was on a low volume, but she could still hear snatches of conversations; something about a big game of some kind, and someone else talking about what they were making for dinner that night.

"Hey, there, Miss, you got a visitor pass?"

Amanda showed him the visitor badge clipped to the hem of her shirt.

"OK, thank you, Miss." He nodded then headed away soon disappearing in an adjacent hallway.

Watching the security guard until he disappeared she finally shook head. "Yup, that's a poor excuse for security. You called it girl," she murmured.

Finally she found the room 128A and, after opening the door, stuck her head inside. The room was large; no doubt it could seat at least fifty people at tables at chairs comfortably. There were no windows and the walls were lined with billboards from famous Broadway shows.

At the front of the room was a row of five occupied wheelchairs in front of which was a raised platform, upon which stood a rail thin brown haired man standing beside a small table where a mini stereo blared music. Amanda recognized the tune being played.

It was a song from the Broadway musical Oklahoma, the one about the fringe on top, or something like that. Her dad loved those musicals and played the cast albums all the time when she was a young girl. But right now she had more important things to take care of, like catching a murderer and helping two ghosts pass over.

One of the occupants of the wheelchairs had to be Milt Spender.

Stepping inside she closed the door as softly as possible so as not to disturb the audiences enjoyment of the show tunes echoing off the walls. She walked as softly as possible toward the platform until she stood behind the wheelchairs, the occupants of which were exclusively male.

How am I going to nail down which one is Spender without interrupting the class?

It was then she noticed the man on the platform was glaring at her his brow marred by deep creases. He was trying to get her attention by mouthing something she didn't understand. She raised her hands in mock surrender and shrugged.

Walking around to stand in front of the wheelchairs she studied each grizzled man. Two were thin, two were heavy, and one was medium. *The three bears of the seniors set.*

One had a scar on his left cheek, one had wispy gray hair that touched his shoulders, and one was bald as a cue ball. Her nose wrinkled at the overpowering odor of garlic emanating from cue ball.

The man at the end of the row glared at her with red-rimmed azure eyes. Unshaven, wearing a dirty, red and brown plaid night gown over sky blue pajamas, his bare feet rested on the foot rests of the wheelchair, he seemed the most likely candidate to be a retired cop. His eyes followed her as she walked toward him. *Yup, cop.*

"Milt?" she whispered after stepping up to stand over him.

He grimaced. "What the fuck do you want?"

His tone suggested aggression, but his hands, buried in his lap, were trembling. And his head wobbled like a bobble head. *Minutiae reveals truth.*

"Let's you and I get out of here, Milt. We need to talk." She sensed all she needed to do was push him a little harder and he'd be putty in her hands.

Milt avoided her steady gaze. "I'm not going anywhere with you, bitch." He spat the words from between his cracked, dry lips, but his words lacked forcefulness.

She moved so she stood in front of him again but he snapped his head in the other direction as if trying to escape. "Really?" she said. "Would you prefer we conducted our *business* in here?"

Milt's eyes shifted to lock with hers. There was fear behind them. "No...I mean...not really..." He reached down to unlock the brake on his chair then began to wheel away using his hands to push the tires forward.

She glanced at the man on the platform and nodded. He raised the index finger of his left hand. *What a nice guy.*

Amanda followed Milt out the door to the corridor then down the hall until they arrived at a door with a picture of him his name written underneath in block letters. The picture of him looked pretty much identical to the man seated in the wheelchair.

Milt slapped a stainless steel plate on the wall next to the door and it began to slowly open into the room. As the gap became wider the florescent lights in the ceiling inside flickered to life.

When the door had opened sufficiently, Milt turned his head slightly to catch her eye, grunted then turned to face forward and rolled himself inside.

Amanda followed him in watching him until he stopped at the window overlooking the golf course where in the distance one gray haired man was striking his golf ball while another man of a similar vintage watched from a powered cart.

It was sunny outside but Milt's room was located under an overhang so very little sunlight came through the window.

Milt's elbows rested on the wheelchairs armrests his hands clasped in front of him, clasping unclasping worrying themselves with nervous energy. He peered at the golfers his body trembling uncontrollably. "I've always knew this day would come," he said, his voice soft as sun warmed butter. "Are you going to kill me now?"

Amanda snorted causing him to look at her surprise registering on his gaunt, unshaven features. "Milt, I'm not here to kill you. I'm here to help Lucy and Gib Dark."

Milt shifted his bottom in his wheelchair. "Gib? Lucy? They're—"

"Dead," she finished for him. "Yes, they are, but their ghosts are very much still around, and they don't want to be *around*, for lack of a term that would make some sense to a lay person such as yourself."

Milt had stopped shaking the fear beginning to dissipate. "Sorry, I don't follow..."

She nodded and moved to sit on the single bed facing him. "Gib claims you killed his wife, Lucy. I need to know if you did." She leaned toward him her eyes on his. "It's just that easy." Now that she was closer she detected the sour smell of sweat coming from Milt. She wondered when was the last time he bathed.

Gib was gaining confidence now his arrogance returning. "I used to be a cop ya know."

She smirked. "Yes, I know. You were Gib's partner." She looked out the window. "From the look of this place I'd say you were a corrupt cop."

Milt's eyes narrowed. "How would you know?"

Amanda chuckled. "Let's stop playing games, Milty, just answer my question; did you murder Lucy Dark?"

"Lady, I have no idea who the *fuck* you are so I'm not gonna tell you shit."

"From what I see, Milt, my boy, you may need my services sooner than later."

"Oh, yeah, really? So who and what are you that a useless old man like me would require your services?"

Amanda grinned. "I'm Amanda Dark, I'm Gib's niece and I'm a paranormal investigator. I also have a special talent helping spirits of the dead unable to cross over after their death due to unresolved issues while they were alive." The grin faded from her lips and she turned her attention to Milt. "You're dying. From your appearance I'd say most likely cancer."

Milt's eyes went wide and watery. "How did you know?"

"I know all, I see all, sorta like a modern day Wizard of Oz, only I don't hide behind a curtain." She paused to consider her next words then she had an idea.

"Listen, Milt, I'll make you a deal, if you tell me who killed Lucy I'll help you cross over when the time comes."

One corner of Milt's mouth curled slightly. "Who said I'd have any problem crossing over?"

"Trust me, Milt, I'm a professional. I always know." Amanda paused to wait for Milt to mull over her offer.

Truth was she had no idea if he'd have problems, she didn't know enough about him. She made her offer on the scant bits of details she'd gleaned after meeting him, her special intuition, and what Gib and Lucy said about him.

It wasn't much to go on, but she was betting even if she missed the mark she'd at least have nicked a corner of truth.

Milt might not actually want to go wherever it was he was headed after death if he was a crooked cop and a murderer. In her experience the after life was never what people expected, or so her spirit contacts told her.

Milt moved his wheelchair slightly back from the window the tires making a soft burr sound on the tiles. His head hung down to his chest. "OK, but please help me. I've done some stuff I'm not proud of..." His voice dropped off and a gasp escaped his lips. He looked up into her eyes trails made by tears ran down his sunken cheeks.

Her heart ached for him. This man suffered from terrible soul crushing pain. She resolved to help him no matter what it took.

"Why don't you tell me everything," she said softly.

In a halting voice Milt began his story.

Amanda listened intent on his words filled with raw emotion concerning things he obviously hadn't talked about in a very long time.

She was right about his terminal cancer. Since Milt was nearing his eighty-ninth birthday he had already accepted the inevitable end.

He assured Amanda he hadn't killed Lucy. Though he was jealous of Gib, and thought Lucy was too good for his partner, he couldn't hurt either of them.

Years after Gib left the police force Milt and his new partner were offered substantial bribes from drug dealers to look the other way.

Since his finances had been wiped out in a real estate scam, and his wife left him, he decided he deserved to retire in style, so he accepted the offers and managed to accrue a significant amount of money. "I was wrong. Money isn't what's important in life," he said.

He then explained that while he didn't kill Lucy he knew who did, but had been threatened with exposure of his corruption if he revealed the truth. He'd remained silent since that time.

Amanda's heart rate increased. Now she was getting somewhere. "Who wanted to send Gib a message by murdering his wife?"

Milt looked down at the floor. "That's what he always believed, but it wasn't true. The killer wasn't sending him any message..." His voice caught.

"OK, so if that wasn't the motive then why?"

Milt sighed his breath shaky. "Someone wanted Lucy for themselves... someone powerful...dangerous. When Gib and Lucy said no he threatened to kill her."

"Who?"

He looked up at her through bloodshot eyes. He opened his mouth to speak but the intercom speaker in the ceiling cut him off. The announcers voice was feminine, nasally, and slightly annoying. "Residents, there are now lemon cookies and green tea available in the cafeteria where we will be starting the bingo game shortly. So join your fellow residents for a full filled afternoon."

As the announcer spoke Amanda stood and walked to the window over looking the golf course her shoes scuffing over the tile.

Watching two new golfers swinging at their balls reminded her what a silly game golf really was.

When announcer had finished she shifted her eyes to look at Milt and froze. His face was the color a concord grape, he gasped for breath, his gnarled hands clasping at his throat.

Her heart beating rapidly, Amanda searched frantically for the call button to summon assistance. Finally her eyes landed on a panel with three colored buttons on the wall over the single bed crammed into an alcove. She hurried to the panel and pressed the black button marked *NURSES STATION*. Nothing happened.

There was a speaker on the panel under the buttons. The label under blue button to the left of the black button said it was for the intercom. Pressing the button and holding it in Amanda shouted into the speaker. "Help! I need help!"

After she released the button a man's sluggish voice replied. "Alright, lady, take it easy."

"No, you don't understand..." Milt had begun to make choking noises and he shuddered as air rushed from his lungs then his eyes rolled back in his head.

Amanda froze her eyes wide with horror as Milt's gnarled hands frantically undid the seat belt holding him in the chair. He tried to stand but instead he slumped forward until finally collapsing to the floor. First on his knees until he dropped on his belly his face bouncing off the tiles with his arms and legs sprawled out from his torso bent at unnatural angles.

Milton Spender was dead.

***

Amanda joined Phillip in the cafeteria where he sat alone at one end of a table large enough for ten people with a cinnamon bun and a white ceramic mug in front of him. Amanda was relieved there were very few people in cafeteria at this time of day since it was just after two o'clock in the afternoon. The last thing she needed was anyone to overhear their conversation then having to explain it. Most people did not understand or appreciate her work.

She could see a few bites were missing from the cinnamon bun but the remainder was untouched. The mug, which she saw contained black coffee, was half empty, or was it half full?

"No good?" she asked nodding at the bun after sitting in an empty chair across from Phillip.

"Terrible," he said, "dry as the dust in a vacuum cleaner bag and the icing is so sweet it hurts your teeth." He shrugged and raised the mug to his lips to take a sip. "Coffee's okay though."

"Milt's dead."

Phillip had raised his mug intending to take another drink of coffee, but stopped a few inches from his mouth the mug floating. "What? How?"

"He was terminal." She shrugged. "It was just a matter of time."

Looking away so he couldn't see the sadness in her eyes she cleared her throat. The truth was she had never gotten used to death no matter how much she experienced in her job. And Milt's end was truly terrible.

She secretly hoped she never would since helping the dead was her motivation to become a paranormal investigator in the first place.

"Wow," said Phillip before he took a generous drink of coffee then set the mug on the table.

"Did he say anything important before he died?"

She nodded still avoiding him. "He said someone else wanted Lucy for themselves, and when she wouldn't agree he threatened to kill her."

"So who was this person?"

Amanda turned to face him and sighed. "He was about to tell me when..."

Phillip snorted and his mouth formed a crooked smile. "Yeah, he was cut off just like in the movies. I'm surprised there wasn't a knife sticking from his back."

"A man is dead, Phillip, this is no time for jokes."

Phillip winced. "Yeah, I'm sorry, Amanda, but death makes me a little goofy. I'll stop. But really, any idea who he might have been talking about?"

She nodded her eyes drifting to the vacant chair next to him then moving back to him. "Actually, there were several gangsters in the trial transcript Gib said may have been the murderer."

Phillip arched a single eyebrow. "Really, any idea, which one Milt might have known?"

"Oh, I expect he knew them all but his ghost told me the name of one who was jealous of Gib and who threatened Lucy."

"Well, why didn't you say so before?"

"Because my dear, Phillip, Milt's ghost just sat down beside you and shared the name with me."

Phillip chuckled. Since partnering with Amanda on several cases nothing shocked him anymore and he fully accepted her talents were very real. "I love it when you use your gift. It really is so cool."

Amanda ginned. "Thanks, partner. We're going to find Al "Stinky" Garbone, the man who allegedly murdered Lucy Dark."

She knew then she didn't need to find Stinky Al because the murder of Lucy was pure cause and effect. Amanda's paranormal senses told her something was rotten in Arizona. Neither Milt nor this faceless small time wise guy, Stinky Al, killed Lucy. She knew now who committed the murder and who should pay the price.

***

Amanda entered the Moonrise Diner with Phillip a step behind her. Upon seeing the diner's interior she pulled up short and he ran into her from behind nearly causing her to stumble and fall. "Hey! Watch it."

"Sorry," Phillip said after stepping away from her. "What's up?"

"Look at this place," Amanda said waving her arms at the pile of wood wreckage around them. It actually seemed worse than before.

Phillip scanned the restaurant. "Yeah, it looks like an old dumpy broken down diner."

Amanda had never expected to find the diner shiny and new like when they left here last time, but the dilapidated condition of the long abandoned building caught her off guard. Dust and mold covered every shattered booth and the rotting counters were weathered and sand blown in through the gaping holes in the walls.

She hadn't realized how bad it was inside before since it had been dark the last time they were here. In the daytime she worried the ceiling would fall on them any second. This wasn't so much a haunted diner as a had-it diner.

"Uhhh, Uncle Gib? Aunt Lucy?" Amanda stepped forward tentatively unsure if the floor might collapse beneath her at any second. She froze when the floorboard under her creaked followed by a loud snapping sound.

Suddenly the broken down restaurant began to transform once again beginning at the far wall.

Amanda closed her eyes as the wave of change came rushing toward her. Her heart pounded hard in her chest. Within seconds there was a soft whirr then a cool breeze washed over her. Opening one eye she saw a smiling Gib standing behind the transformed lunch counter beside Lucy who also grinned at her.

"Whew," she said, "I'm so glad to see you two." Amanda collapsed with relief on an empty stool while Phillip sat on the one next to her. She shot him a glance and saw he his eyes looked as relieved as she felt. The diner had been regenerated before it fell on them.

"Do you have good news?" asked Gib, his handsome face eager as a child on his birthday.

"Sort of," began Amanda uncertain how Gib and Lucy would accept the death of his old partner. Much like taking off a Band Aid it was best to pull it off in one go. "Milt's dead."

Gib's face sagged. "Really?"

Amanda nodded. "But I did manage to speak to him while he was still alive."

"So you killed him?" said Lucy as she wiped the counter with a white cloth.

"No, of course not, I don't kill people. I just talk to dead people." She hesitated realizing how ridiculous this sounded. But then Gib and Lucy were ghosts and she was talking to them.

Gib glanced at Lucy. "Why don't you get them some coffee?" Lucy nodded and walked to the stainless steel coffee brewer station standing on the service counter in front of the wall separating the kitchen from the counter area. The brewer had three warmers each with a glass carafe containing black coffee.

The two on the side warmers were half full; the one under the dispensing spout was three quarters full.

Ghosts must drink a lot of coffee.

Lucy filled two white ceramic mugs then came back to set them on the lunch counter in front of them. "I'll get the creamer and the sugar," she said. She quickly returned with a stainless steel creamer with a hinged lid, a mint green ceramic bowl filled with white sugar, and two spoons.

Phillip looked at Amanda his eyes curious. She shrugged then reached to grasp the mug and realized it was warm. Raising the mug she sipped the coffee and it tasted slightly nutty and rich. How was this possible?

Lucy looked anxious. "Is it OK?"

Amanda nodded. "Yeah, it's good." Phillip raised his mug and took a small sip. His eyes went wide.

Amanda grinned and set the mug back on the counter. "As I was saying I spoke to Milt and he told me who really murdered Lucy." Seeing the fear in Gib's ghostly eyes she paused. It seemed every case brought new experiences. *A ghost afraid? Who knew?*

She cleared her throat then continued. "Anyway, Milt says some guy named Stinky Al murdered Lucy—"

"I knew it!" Gib cut her off and turned to face his wife. "You and Al? Really?"

Lucy took two steps back from Gib her body trembling fear in her eyes. "Gib, it wasn't like that..."

Gib walked up to her and pressed an index finger into her chest "Really? You and Al were cheating on me behind my back, weren't you? You lousy whore! Slut!" It was then Amanda realized Gib had a chef's knife gripped in his right hand. He stepped up and slashed the blade across Lucy's throat.

Since she was a ghost her head separated from her body floating in mid air, but no blood came from the wound. "Gib!" Lucy's disembodied head screamed at her husband. "You bastard! You killed me again."

Amanda leaned closer to Phillip in order not to be heard. "I think it's time we exited stage left."

Phillip raised one eyebrow. "Huh?"

"Let's go and leave these two lovebirds alone."

They rose simultaneously from the stools and hurried to the door just as the diner began to change to its former state of about to collapse.

Once outside they watched as the diner's four walls collapse inward with a loud crash. Then the roof fell onto the pile of broken, weather-grayed wood enveloping them in a cloud of dust and sand. The diner was now a pile of kindling.

"What just happened?" said Phillip coughing as the dust cloud settled over them. Trying in vain to brush off his tan shorts and cactus green shirt he turned to face Amanda who shook her head to shake some of the dust out of her hair.

She snorted to clear her nostrils and spat sand from her mouth. "The end of the Moonrise Diner obviously, but also the truth."

"What truth?"

"Gib killed Lucy and got away with it. Blaming Milt then Stinky Al, they were decoys, or maybe an excuse to fool himself, or to bury his guilt, or who knows why. Whatever the reasons, my Uncle Gib is exactly who he appeared to be."

"What now?"

Amanda smirked. "Well, I expect with the destruction of the diner they've both crossed over."

She scanned the wreckage. "Somehow I don't think Gib is much liking where he ended up."

Phillip stepped up and wrapped his arms around her. She hugged him back feeling his heart beating against her chest. "What about you?" he said softly.

"I'm better. Much better."

Whoever said the truth will set you free knew exactly what they were talking about because Amanda Dark had never felt as free as she did right now.

This idea for this story originates in Genesis Chapter 3 verse 4. Many chapters in the Bible abound with mysteries this tale tried to explain what happened after.

Heroes of Old

WE ARE THE HEROES OF OLD, MEN OF RENOWN; at least that's what some say about us. Others hate us. They are trying to kill us.

"Nick!" I shout over the sounds of pulse rifle blasts coming from a shattered building east of our position. It's exterior is peppered with charred holes resulting from heavy weapons fire. The interior of my enviro-suit's coated with my own sour sweat. I smell dreadful, even to me. A layer of dust covering the faceplate impairs my vision more than I will admit. Seeing the location of the enemy is a challenge.

The charge icon on my heads-up display on my side of the helmet faceplate is glowing; indicating I have two hours remaining before recharging is mandatory. The atmosphere indicator next to the energy icon shows the available air will run out before then anyway.

My bigger problem is I have been unable to contact anyone outside the battle zone, not even the twenty other troopers we had attacked with. No one's responding to my hail and this worries me.

My first command and I've screwed it up.

"Yeah, Turn! I'm here."

Nick's voice came from somewhere to my left possibly behind the single standing wall of a shattered dwelling. His com-link must be knocked out since his voice echoed across the rubble field between us not from my suit's comm.

"I'm coming to you. Stay where you are," I call back. Not waiting for his acknowledgement I crouch low then wait until several energy bolts pass overhead, I plan to break for his position when the enemy adjusts their targeting scanners trying to reacquire us.

Sucking in a breath, clutching my weapon to my chest, I run into the open rushing in the direction of where I hope Nick is holed up behind the wall.

A bolt of superheated energy shoots overhead missing me by less than a meter. My suit's alarm rang in my ears as the heat penetrates the layers of protection between certain death and me. My death is inconsequential to the overall plan for Noah III, and besides I know where I'm headed after death. Heaven will be glorious, but He needed me here and now. As long as I'm able to draw a breath I will fight for the Holy commission.

My rapid breathing echoed in ears and salty sweat streaming off my forehead made seeing clearly difficult. My suit's internal cooling unit may have failed when I took a glancing hit from a blaster. I've been inside this suit for three days. Stale sweat and unwashed me isn't a pleasant combination on my senses. But I can't remove the suit until I return to base. The thin air of Noah III makes physical operations difficult for humans. This is where the enemy has the advantage over us.

At the pre-mission briefing, Senior-Level Trooper Joshua stated the enemy, while as human as we, have occupied this planet for over five millennia so they have acclimated to the heat and atmospheric conditions hundreds of years ago.

It nagged deep in my soldier's brain that command should have been better prepared us for these conditions. The planet has turned out to be a meat grinder.

I finally arrive at the wall where I hope to find Nick and manage to sprawl onto my belly behind it just as an enemy sniper's shot passes through where I had just been. Unfortunately I landed on a mound of jagged rubble cutting into my body sending searing pain through me.

I groan as I roll off the rubble onto my back and my gloved fingers loosen around the stock of my blast rifle and it slid out of my hand. Unable to hold it my rifle rattles across the shattered stones as my grip releases until it finally stops when it comes to rest somewhere below me out of my line of sight. My chest burns and my mouth tastes of coppery blood. There is a sharp pain as I involuntarily lick my lips. Evidently my lip has split open and blood now flows down my chin.

Dizziness gripped me but I manage to glance to my left. There I discover Nick sitting with his back against the wall his left leg torn and bleeding below the knee. His suit has closed around the gash in the fabric, as it was designed to, but his blood surrounds him like a red halo. His cloudy, half-closed eyes look at me. We're both in a bad way. For the first time since we joined the Order of Seth together over a decade ago I'm unsure we will make it home.

Looking up at the expanse of slate gray sky dotted with billowing muddy clouds overhead I swallow hard and move my right hand to my chest then down my body. Spots danced before my vision when my fingers brush something that sends sharp pains through my badly mangled body. I realize what has happened. I've broken more than one rib and something protrudes through the left side of my chest.

I'm not dead so whatever it hit me missed my heart, but my situation is not good. Not good at all.

I wince as I steal another glance again at Nick. I conclude he doesn't look in much better shape than me. We need help. Fast.

Reaching for the cover over the control panel affixed to the right arm of my enviro-suit I press the recessed button that flips the panel open. When it opens I press the Emergency Beacon with one gloved finger. This will dispatch a strike force to pound the area we're in with heavy ordnance. Now, the kicker is if Nick and I don't move to cover within the next forty-five seconds we will be vaporized along with the enemy, civilians, and the remainder of my squad if any are still alive.

And I will be responsible it will be my failure. EB is the option of last resort.

Our cause is Holy and just, so it will succeed. Everyone will die.

The Sons of Noah are terrorists who deserve to die for their cause and actions. Of course their cause is unclear even though from their propaganda over the past fifty-two years it has been clear they are evil incarnate. At least that's what I've been told since childhood.

I'm just not certain of the truth anymore. Too often doubts crept into my thoughts during the cold, hungry nights on the battlefield. Imminent death makes a man think.

For my own satisfaction, and to erase the doubts, I hoped during this mission to capture one of the Sons so I could question him or her directly. I'm going native; I just want to be certain, or as certain as I can be, of our motivation. Regardless I am a soldier. I follow orders. I will still kill the enemy if ordered to do so. I prayed the order itself is just.

Reaching for the controls on my suit I press the medical evac call button, which will dispatch a rescue transport. The transports aren't allowed to enter an active battle zones so it will hover near the edge of the carnage until I signal we are alive. The transports crew will conduct routine life scans regardless, but my second signal will give them an epicentre to start the search for survivors.

I study the shredded wall Nick rests against my eyes travelling from the top to the bottom. I knew what I must do. The wall will provide the cover from the ordnance blast we need but it will need to be on top of us if we were to survive. Our odds of surviving being buried were slim, but the destruction of the neighbourhood will kill us for sure so any chance is better than none.

Struggling to sit, I fight through nauseating pain until I finally manage to sit upright. It feels like I'm swimming under water, the air feels thick as cream. While blowing shallow breaths and gritting my teeth I struggled to my knees. My head was swimming and I swallowed vomit surging from my stomach up my throat.

Looking down I see a piece of wood sticking from the left side of my chest. My rifle lay on the ground to my right. After considering reaching for the gun I realize time is far too short for me to get to the weapon. We need to find cover right now.

I drop forward onto my hands and knees then, grunting with effort and fighting through searing pain, I crawled over the uneven ground to get to Nick. After what seemed like an eternity I'm beside him. He's conscious but delusional. He moans and shakes his head side to side as if trying clear his mind from a fog. Through his faceplate I see his eyes are narrow, the brown pupils small. His dusky features are shiny with sweat. Out of the corner of one eye I see what I am hoping to find. Next to him lay his blast rifle, intact and fully charged. My heart rate increases.

We still had a chance.

"Don't move," says a deep voice over my comm I'm unable to clearly identify as male or female. I look over my shoulder and there stands a Son of Noah soldier in its orange and black armour. The business end of a pulse rifle is aimed at my chest. The stylized bright red humanoid-shaped logo over his left breast with what appears to be devils horns. According to the pre-mission briefings this tells me this is a senior leader within its command structure. It seems odd to send a senior to kill grunts like us but right now this is the last thing on my mind.

I try to swallow but my mouth and throat are dry as desert sand. I don't fear death, but I worry for Nick. He hasn't accepted his role in creation not has he accepted the superiority of the great I Am. His death will be blood on my hands, not this Son of Noah's.

I turn to face this enemy. If I'm to die then I want to see my killer. "Mid-Level Trooper Judah Turner unit number D889871," I say as I've been trained to do when captured. I pause awaiting the inevitable sting of a full force pulse blast designed to end my mortal life. I utter a short prayer under my breath.

"I'm not going to kill either of you," replies the enemy solider as it lowers its weapon until it points toward the ground.

I consider going for Nick's gun but decide differently when three additional Sons of Noah appear from behind the standing over us each hefting serious firepower. This is when the pain I had been fighting finally won and the war torn world around me drops into blackness. My last thought before losing consciousness is to wonder what happened to our strike force.

Little did I know this would be the first of many unanswered questions.

***

I have no sense of time when my eyes flutter open. The sudden brightness forces me to squeeze them shut. I gasp for air as a wave of dizziness and nausea threatens to overwhelm me. The sour taste of bile fills my mouth and nose.

"It's OK. Rest easy." The voice has a feminine softness to it, but this was the voice of an enemy no one has ever seen unless the Emergency Evac shuttle had picked us up.

I tense. Nick. Where's Nick? I slowly open my eyes again and blink away the brightness until I can make out the human form leaning over me. As my sight returns I recognize the form isn't human at all. It's a machine. An artificial being.

The head is round and made from some sort of silver-gray, smooth burnished metal. What I can make up of the chest and torso the machine's body is unclothed and made of the same material as the head. It has a slit where the eyes would be on a human and it has four limbs. I realize I lying in soft bed in a snow white room with no windows. I'm not wearing my enviro-suit yet I can breathe comfortably. I sniff the air and detect a faint metallic odour of machine oil.

"Where am I?" My voice is strange, raspy.

The machine's head swivelled from where it had been studying a readout display screen on the wall beside my bed to look at me. The slit seemed to stare at me making me vaguely uneasy.

"How do you feel, sir?" Its voice is machine like, robotic.

I want to move but somehow I know if I did the pain would be excruciating. I decide it best to play the confused guy, for now. "No idea actually. I'm weak, confused. I...where am I? Where's Nick?"

87

"Don't worry, sir, your companion, in fact all your companions, are fine."

The machine spoke so casually almost as if my troopers had merely stubbed their toes. I knew differently.

This machine is telling me my trooper survived the battle. How is this possible? I recall requesting the bombardment. I sucked in a breath. No. Impossible.

I try to move my legs and arms only to realize I'm restrained.

"Why am I tied up?"

"For your safety, sir," replied the machine. With these words the machine left my bedside its track system whirring as it moved. I turn my head in time to witness a blank wall suddenly slide aside then the machine disappear into a plain white corridor beyond the newly created doorway then the wall slid shut.

I'm alone. I swallow hard. What next? What's going to happen to me?

As if reading my mind the wall opened again to admit a man. At least he looked like a man. His short blond hair, blue eyes, and pale skin seemed far too human for a Son of Noah. No one had seen one in person yet I always had the impression they are far more alien in appearance.

"Hello." He smiles as he speaks and his blue eyes are bright, his voice gentle. He wears a simple white jumpsuit and carries a data pad. "My name's, Dr. Bolt. I'd like to check your vitals and hopefully answer any questions you may have."

Finally, answers. "Where am I and who are you people?"

Dr. Bolt hugs the data pad to his chest and looks directly in the eye making me oddly uncomfortable. His brow wrinkles slightly. "Those are good questions.

I'm sure the AI already told you your friends are fine and in good health, or at least okay for now. They are in rooms much like this one under my care."

He pauses and his eyes drift to the wall monitor where my vital signs are displayed in glowing red and yellow lettering against a sky blue background. I have no idea how to read the data, but from Bolt's expression I knew I have no cause for concern. At least not with my health. My future hasn't been written.

Bolt's eyes drifts back to lock with mine. A tight humourless smile played across his lips. "You are in a secure military hospital outside the city your comrades just flattened." The smiled melted away as his eyes hardened. "A lot of lives were lost. Mostly civilian."

I thought about his words for several seconds. "I'm sorry. But war is a dirty business but if the cause is just then any lives lost is not in vein."

Bolt dismisses my words with a wave of his right hand his left still hugging the data pad. "I'm not a political person. I'm a healer. My orders are to ensure you and your troopers recover from your wounds so you can stand trial."

Trial?

"I'm a soldier not a terrorist. Under galactic convention I am a prisoner of war and entitled to fair treatment as such."

Bolt emits a soft laugh and shakes his head. "I'm also not a legal expert. If you wish to take up the issue with your advocate she will be here shortly."

"Oh, sorry, doctor." He is right of course. I need an advocate. Taking in a deep breath fighting the sudden surge of anger burning in my belly.

The Sons of Noah devastated our colonies across the galaxy, killed billions of our citizens, and they wish to charge us for defending God's chosen people? Outrageous.

"Uhhhh, thank you for your help, doctor. I certainly feel better than when I was wounded during the battle."

He nods then shifts his attention to keying something on his data pad. Finally he finishes. I detect the scent of cinnamon coming from him. I must be bored.

"OK, everything seems fine. I'll be back later to check on you. Do you require anything?" I shake my head. Without responding Bolt disappears into the hallway beyond the doorway, as the android nurse had before him, then the wall slid into place behind him with a barely discernable thump.

I stare at the white sterile ceiling listening to my heartbeat steadily and close my eyes. I pray for forgiveness for my failure in the silence. My sense of time is skewed. I am unable to say how much time passed before the wall opens again. This time a well-dressed woman enters the room. She wears her dark hair tied into a ponytail her features are angular, her brown eyes blood webbed with dark shadows under them, from lack of sleep. The doorway closes behind her. We're alone.

A chair appears through a panel opening in the floor next to my bed. It locks into place with a click. Her eyes avoid mine as she sits in the chair her pale hands smoothing the fabric of her steel gray jumpsuit. She sighs and I detect the stale odour of garlic on her breath.

I suddenly realize my stomach is knotted by hunger. "You are my advocate?"

After clearing her throat her eyes finally looked into mine.

The only way I can describe her expression is the deadpan look of a poker player, which may be the most apt description of a legal advocates role.

"Yes, Mr. Turner, I am going to be aiding in your defence at your trial. My name's Alva Dix."

I open my mouth intending to protest her using my civilian honorific rather than my rank until she raises one hand stopping me from speaking.

"Before you correct my failure to recognize your rank as a soldier I have to tell you your government refuses to acknowledge you and your squads military connection to them in any way. They have disavowed you and claim you and your troopers are rogues and mercenaries working for a terrorist former general of your army."

My heart stops and time freezes. This can't be. We were operating under authorized orders. It suddenly dawns on me I know what has happened. I swallow hard fighting the knot of anger and disgust that invades my body. "Peace. Our governments reached a peace agreement. Right?"

She nods. "The general was executed two days ago."

Oh, my Lord, my life is over. My government has deserted my soldiers and me. But as my senior trainer once told me, "Where there is life there is hope."

"Do my troopers have any chance?"

The advocate avoids my eyes before she speaks again. "Yes, if you accept sole responsibility for the attack on Nephilim City and sign a confession to that effect your troopers will receive reduced sentences."

I swallowed again. "How reduced?"

"They won't be executed. Life in prison. Parole after twenty years is the usual restriction."

After a brief pause she added, "Of course they have to survive prison."

"And I will be executed, correct?" Her gaze shifts to look at me. She nods.

Well there it is. I will become a martyr for the honour of my troopers, my race, and most importantly, for the great I Am.

I close my eyes and suck in a breath. Death did not worry me. The day I fought in my first battle I expected to die. After many battles, some of which I'd been seriously wounded but somehow survived to continue the Holy War, I'd been close to death so many times I'd lost count. Today my role in the Holy commission is now coming to an end.

"OK, advocate. I will plead guilty provided they allow my troopers to live. And if they allow them to be exchanged as prisoners of war."

She shook her head. "No, they will not accept those terms. The troopers are terrorists not enemy combatants."

I smile at her. "They can and they will. They want to hold someone accountable for the war between the Order of the Seth and the Sons of Noah and that someone is me. I accept that, but I alone must be the one to be martyred. Otherwise they will have to execute all of us and how would that look?"

Her eyes went wide with surprise as if something I'd struck a nerve. "You think you've been captured by the Sons of Noah? Is that who you think you've been fighting?"

"Yes, for a decade."

"No. I don't know who told you that but you've been seriously misinformed." Anger rose in her voice with each word. "These are the Nephilim who fled to Earth thousands of years ago.

The Order of Seth has been trying to exterminate them since that time."

I suddenly realize everything I've ever been taught is wrong. This war has never been a Holy mission. It is a lie perpetrated by evil. I need to pray for forgiveness.

***

The guards escort me to the disintegration chamber. I am resigned to my destiny. I hoped to die in the line of fire but it is not to be my path home. My body will be consumed in a sudden burst of super heated energy releasing my soul to heaven.

My advocate stood beside the door to the chamber. She gazes at me her eyes reflecting regret. "I'm sorry," she says, "I tried my best."

I smile at her. "No need to feel sorry, Advocate Dix, I'm at peace with my decision. I look forward to being united with God's Kingdom."

Her features relax and her shoulders slump. I am pleased my last act in this world is to comfort someone.

I step into the open door of the disintegrator and the door closes behind me. I suck in a breath and held with my eyes closed. Death will be quick and painless.

Nothing. Several seconds went by and when nothing happened I open my eyes just as the door opens. I blink unable to process what I'm seeing.

Before me are green rolling hills, blue sky stretching to the horizon. I'm startled when a bird shoots past the open door. I sniff the air. Jasmine, fresh cool air, and water.

Hesitantly I step through the door. "Paradise," I murmur under my breath.

"No, not really," says a familiar voice.

Looking to my left I discover Nick sitting on the grass. He wears a simple gray jumpsuit and his feet are bare. My heart beats hard and I almost drop to my knees as the joy at seeing him alive and well threatens to overwhelm me. "Nick! What the—"

Nick snorts dismissively. "Don't even go there, Turn. You sent us here. We're stuck in this paradise as you call it." His features morphed as his scowl deepened.

"We?"

"Yes, me and the troopers from our unit. We've been exiled here. Stranded."

Raising my hands in mock surrender I take a step toward him. He nails me with a glare so I come to an abrupt halt. "Listen, Nick, I have no idea what you're talking about." Studying the landscape around us dotted with brilliant orange, red, and purple flowers to name a few, I add, "Besides this place doesn't look so awful."

"It doesn't, huh? Well, Mr. Turner, we're soldiers. The nearest war must be light years away from here. Where ever here is."

Now all had been revealed. My advocate is a phony, the offer was a phony, and my troopers and I have been quarantined on this planet far from home, and far from the war. But for what reason?

"What did they promise you, Nick?"

He avoids my gaze and a smirk passed over his rugged features. The scar running down his right cheek to his stubble covered chin pales. "An advocate told me if I gave them the launch coordinates for our fire base so they could destroy our chemical weapons stockpile they would send you home. And of course I would be executed which seemed like a great deal to me. Since the war was over and all."

"But the war wasn't over was it?"

He shook his head. We had been duped. I sank to the sun warmed grass and began to sob. I failed my people and my God.

We were no longer the heroes of old, the men of renown. We were nothing.

In the near future we will no doubt discover the truth about the mythical Sasquatch than wanders in our western wooden. This tale provides one possible truth.

It's A Small Galaxy

SHEILA CULPEPPER YAWNED AS SHE SHUFFLED across the cool ceramic tiles on the kitchen floor toward the door to the pantry. The kitchen cupboard where they kept her favorite full-fiber breakfast cereal was again empty.

Her grey eyes drifted toward Bernie, her husband of fifteen years, sitting on a burnished steel stool, topped with a crimson, mushroom-shaped cushion, his narrow shoulders hunched over as he read the morning news on the virtual screen hovering over the speckled granite island. A half-eaten bowl of her cereal floating in a bath of almond milk sat untouched on the island to his left. She rolled her eyes. He wasted more than he ate.

Will Bernie ever remember to restock the cupboards or will I be doing this for the rest of my days? she wondered. Her attention shifted to the cupboard door.

"Open," she said, pulling her robe tighter about her narrow waist.

The door slide aside and she froze. Was she seeing things? She pinched her arm and it hurt, so she wasn't dreaming. She eyed the thing blocking the shelf of cereal, rice, and dried pasta. *What the hell is this?*

97

Inside the pantry was a tall creature—no other words came to mind to describe it—covered head to toe in matted brown hair. It's inky gaze was unfocussed and its mouth hung open, revealing razor sharp teeth both top and bottom of the snout-like jaw. It didn't appear to be wearing clothing; the hair covering its body obscured any anatomical details.

She shot Bernie a disparaging look over her left shoulder. "Bernie," she said between gritted teeth, her tone sharp as a new shaving razor.

He either didn't hear her or was ignoring her on purpose, his eyes still narrow and focused on what she could make out from across the island was an article on celestial mechanics as they related to the new interstellar propulsion system being developed by GenY Astro Nav Corporation.

Him and his damned engines.

She'd always wondered why the most gifted, award-winning bioengineer in the galaxy wasted his free time studying rocket jockey crap. All he ever said was he liked to tinker with engines. Her mandar told her his explanations were evasive, but his love of rockets was the one part of his life he refused to share with her. At least until the hair suit giant showed up the cupboard. Now Bernie had two secrets and she didn't like it one bit.

"Bernie!"

Though she hated raising her voice, she'd finally gained his attention. He looked at her, his mouth hanging open, his azure eyes wide registering a look of surprise dusted with a modicum of impatience. His black curled hair was askew, looking as if it had been pressed to one side on his oval head. He was dressed in a slate gray, short-sleeved tee shirt and matching sports shorts—his usual bedtime attire.

"What?" he said. "I'm busy. I—" He stopped short, his mouth hanging open when he noticed the reddish hue born of anger on Sheila's face, and her fiery glare.

Sheila stepped aside to reveal the huge hairy beast in the pantry behind her—she decided to try out different descriptions to see how they sounded. Unfortunately, beast didn't sound as good a description as creature; it didn't seem to fit. Creature seemed more apropos.

His face flushed the colour of the stoplight at the corner of oh-oh and aw, crap. "Uhhh...listen, Sheila. I'm sorry. I should have told you..." His words petered out.

"Did your father drop this *thing* off?" (Thing seemed a worthy contender for a description.)

Bernie nodded.

"When?"

Bernie's father, Jules, was always bringing over some piece of crap (Jules and Bernie called them treasures, she called them crap) he discovered at flea markets and yard sales.

"Yesterday."

"Well, what is it and what are we supposed to do with it?"

Bernie instructed the virtual screen to turn off, climbed off the stool, and walked to her, his bare feet padding in the quiet kitchen. As he reached her, then gripped the sides of her shoulders and gazed into her eyes, his look said something she hadn't seen before. Her heart went out to her beloved husband. She hated to see him in pain.

"What's wrong?" she asked, her voice barely above a whisper.

"My dad's terminally ill and he's decided to let a few things go before..." His words caught in his throat and his eyes welled with tears. Shelia stepped up and enveloped him in her arms. He shuddered as a sob escaped his lips.

She could feel his heart beating faster and the warmth of him, and the remnants of his aftershave from yesterday filled her nostrils, the odor reminding her of the beach where they used to go for family picnics with Jules when their kids were little. A deep sense of sadness fell over her. She'd lost her own parents in a car crash before the fully-automated driver control system had been developed; now she would be losing Jules, too.

Bernie's mother had died during a deep space research mission years ago when Bernie was in his late teens. Jules had lived alone for the past seventy years.

Shaking off the feelings caused by the memories that had surfaced, she realized she didn't recall seeing a giant, hair-covered creature in Jules garage or anywhere in his three-bedroom bungalow in West Vancouver. Given the size of the thing, it would have been hard to miss.

Finally she released Bernie and took a step back to gaze into his teary eyes. "I'm so sorry about Jules," she said in a low voice. "But it still doesn't explain the big hair-ball in our pantry."

Bernie's chin slumped to his chest. "Dad once brought home a science kit as a present when he returned from an off world business trip. I was ten."

"I don't understand," Sheila said.

"The kit was an alien bioengineering toy designed for their children to learn how to make clones."

Sheila's eyes went wide and her heart beat faster as the implications of what her husband was saying sank in. "You mean you made a *real* Sasquatch?"

Bernie wiped his eyes with the back of one hand and nodded sheepishly. "I named him Shakespeare...and I referred to him as a Bigfoot rather than the more correct first nations name."

He avoided her by looking out the sliding glass door overlooking the sunshine-soaked pool in the backyard. He shrugged. "To a ten-year-old, Bigfoot sounds cooler than Sasquatch."

Sheila shook her head in wonder. She thought for a second, then realized something important. "But no one's ever found a living Bigfoot or Sasquatch...whatever." This conversation was fast sinking into the ridiculous zone.

Bernie shifted to look at her, his eyes reflecting growing excitement. If this had been one of his deep secrets, he certainly appeared happy to share it now. "That's the big thing about this...uh, *toy* I made. I used DNA extracted from Bigfoot droppings from the Sasquatch museum near Squamish."

"Okay, so Shakespeare is a toy and your dad kept him to gather dust until, now, he's dropped it off for you." Sheila pondered her words for a moment. "What are we going to do with it?"

"With what?" said a voice from the entryway into the kitchen. It was Ryder, their eleven-year-old son. He entered, still dressed in his navy-blue shorts and white tee shirt, his narrow feet encased in his favourite fuzzy slippers.

Sheila turned toward her son and smiled. "Morning, Ryder, how'd you sleep?"

The towheaded boy, his pale green eyes roaming the room, padded across the tiled floor until he suddenly froze and his eyes became wide as saucers, staring openmouthed at the tall, hairy creature inside the open pantry.

"What is that?" he asked, his voice filled with wonder. Clearly, he wasn't afraid. His eyes relaxed and he started forward, but before he got too close, Sheila grabbed his arm and restrained him.

She was still unsure if the beast (*maybe beast was a good word?*) was dangerous.

101

It may have been Bernie's toy when he was a boy, but the creature was massive and those razor-sharp teeth could probably rip flesh from bones.

Bernie chuckled, surprising her. She looked at her husband. He wore a wide smile on his angular features and his right hand covered his mouth.

"What's so funny?" she asked. "Your toy could be dangerous to small children."

Bernie laughed. "Don't be ridiculous, Sheila. Shakespeare's been in stasis for over forty years."

"His name's Shakespeare?'" interrupted Ryder.

Bernie moved to stand beside Ryder and draped one long arm across his son's shoulders, curling his hand around Ryder's other arm, hugging him closer. "Yes, Ry, he's a Bigfoot. He was my favourite toy when I was about your age."

"Where did he come from? And why haven't we seen him before?"

Bernie grinned in obvious pride. "I made him. And Grandpa needed to clear our a few things so he woke him up."

Ryder looked up at his father and frowned as one eyebrow arched on his forehead. "Com'on, Dad, you're kiddin' me, right?"

Bernie chuckled. "No, son, not at all. Grandpa gave me a science kit from another planet and I used it to clone him."

Ryder shrugged. "Okay...I guess..."

Sheila saw the doubt in Ryder's eyes and smiled to herself. Ryder was the brightest kid in his pre-med class and it took a lot, even for a genius like her husband, to put one over on their son.

"Anyone gonna ask me?" The voice was deep and loud in the confines of the pantry cupboard.

Slowly Sheila turned to face the creature...the word *monster* suddenly popped into her mind. *Monster...perfect.*

Bernie released Ryder and entered the pantry cupboard. "Hey, Shakespeare, no see long time." The monster laughed, sounding more like a roaring, ravenous lion than a cryptid creation of her husband's manufacture.

Sheila's heart beat more rapidly, and for the first time since seeing the monster in the pantry (*Hey, not a bad title for my next article*), she worried they might be in danger.

But she relaxed when she saw the monster had wrapped its long arms around her husband's slim body and lifted him off his feet in a bear hug. The sounds of what was obviously two old friends laughing and muttering unintelligible words of friendship made Sheila feel a little left out.

"Hey, you two," she called, "get a room." She crossed her arms over her chest.

Out of the corner of one eye, she saw Ryder had walked to the cupboard where the cereal was stored where he, too, discovered it was empty. Her stomach growled to remind her she hadn't eaten breakfast yet.

"Listen, Bernie and...."

"Shakespeare," said the monster, his round, beady eyes gazing at her from above Bernie's head. At least she now had a way to measure the size of him. Bernie was almost two meters tall and the creature towered over him, so she realized he had to be at least two and half meters tall.

She offered him a tight smile. She wasn't about to become fast friends with this creature until she knew more about him, and more about his relationship with her husband. Right now, she knew nothing about him.

***

After Sheila and Ryder had finished breakfast, they joined Bernie and Shakespeare in the living room, where they had retreated while she and her son ate.

Two boxes of cereal were missing from the pantry shelf, so she assumed the creature—she reminded herself she better use the name Bernie had given the Bigfoot or risk embarrassing herself or Bernie. Truthfully, she didn't care about the monster's feelings. She didn't even know if he had feelings, at least as a human being might understand them.

In the past two hundred years since trade with alien worlds had become more widespread, she had met all sorts of aliens with manners ranging from indifference toward humans to rude to overly—almost intrusively so—friendly; so until she had more time to know him (assuming it really was a *him*), Shakespeare would have to prove himself to her.

Bernie was far too enamoured with his childhood plaything to be honest with her or with himself about the creature. As far as she was concerned, her primary duty was protecting her son. But even Ryder appeared to have become infatuated with Shakespeare. Sheila had to tell him three times not to wolf down his breakfast as if he were a wild animal. He was so excited by the sudden appearance of the two-and-a-half-meter-tall Bigfoot.

After breakfast the boy tore into the living room ahead of her to join the Bigfoot and his father. Rolling her eyes, she walked to the front room feeling edgy, with butterflies definitely not flying in formation in her stomach. She didn't know why Shakespeare made her nervous but he did.

104

She found the Bigfoot sitting on the pink and mint-green couch, the cushion mashed flat from his weight—which had to be considerable given his size—and Bernie sat in one of the matching big wing chairs bracketing the couch, laughing. Ryder sat next to Shakespeare. The creature had one hand the size of a baseball glove wrapped around her son's shoulder, hugging him in to his hairy side. The boy's youthful features were split by a wide smile and his inner joy had traveled to his eyes.

Sheila moved across the room and sat on the other wing chair. She watched her son and smiled to herself. He was enjoying meeting his father's childhood toy and listening to their tales of those days. She froze when she heard Shakespeare say something about detectives and it clearly wasn't fictional sleuths.

Bernie had talked about wanting to be a detective as long as she'd known him. All those cheesy ancient stories he read from the net library on his virtual reader about crime and detectives, and those old films he watched every Saturday even when they were dating twenty years ago. She always thought it was his boyhood fantasies. Now here was this childhood toy monster talking about detectives.

"Excuse me, Bernie and...uhhh...Shakespeare. I have a question?" Sheila said, causing three sets of eyes to turn in her direction, including two inky eyes surrounded by bushy hair the colour of her ginger cat. "Ummm...what's this about detectives?"

Shakespeare exchanged a look with Bernie, then the creature began to explain. "After Bernie made me and I had grown to the equivalent of a human teenager, about two years—" Sheila's expression must have been sceptical because the creature stopped to clarify. "Bigfoot's," the creature paused and his snout wrinkled, "or is it Bigfeet?" Shakespeare shook his head.

"Anyway, when I was a teenager, Bernie and I decided to become detectives and solve crimes. Ya know, missing pets, break-ins, thefts from backyards. Relatively minor stuff. We didn't want any money for helping out our neighbors, it was purely problem solving. Ya know, fun." Shakespeare laughed in his growly voice.

Bernie's eyes became serious. Sheila's body tensed as a knot formed in her stomach. Her husband rarely showed his serious side at home. It kind of turned her on.

Shakespeare continued. "That was until an old man in the neighborhood went missing. We didn't get involved until the police and the neighborhood had conducted a thorough search for him and then eventually called it off."

"What's his name?" asked Ryder.

Shakespeare hugged the boy closer to him. "Min Bakster."

Ryder's brow wrinkled and his eyes became curious. "That's a funny name."

Shakespeare chuckled. "I didn't buy the story myself and tried to convince Bernie it was a neighborhood kid pulling our legs." He cleared his nose with a loud *whuff*, startling Sheila. The sounds coming out of this creature were *so* loud.

Oddly, Ryder and Bernie seemed unfazed. Of course, they often attended the indoor sky car races and the cars' engines were loud, so higher than normal decibel levels didn't bother them. Sheila saw no point to watching sky cars going round and round, but she had her own hobbies they didn't care much about. Sewing flags, gardening, and water filtration engineering were what she enjoyed.

But, seeing the look of pure joy on her son's features and the twinkle in his eyes, she decided to play along with this ridiculous story. Shakespears brow wrinkled and he seemed deep in thought.

"Why don't we ask Min Bakster if he knows where the Cruz kid is now?"

Bernie shrugged. "It's been over forty years...he may have moved away or something. I haven't lived in the old neighbourhood for decades..."

"But, Dad, isn't your parents' house under water?" asked Ryder, his excitement bubbling over in his voice.

Bernie cast Ryder a wry smile. "Yeah, you're right, of course, Ryder. Richmond is under sixteen meters of ocean. We could look for Bakster on the net."

Shakespeare stood, towering over them. "Great idea. Let's find out where Old Man Bakster is now. " He moved to the big screen on the wall over the ice stone fireplace, apparently looking for the *on* button or the remote. No one used such old technology anymore, but he had been in stasis for forty years. Sheila understood immediately and decided to help the poor creature. Being out of the familiar could be quite unsettling.

She stood and walked to stand beside the mountain of ginger hair. "Things have changed since you went into the deep freeze, Shakespeare." She patted his arm. Surprisingly, his fur was soft to the touch. "Screen on. Net," she said, facing the wide screen.

The digital screen came on with the Peach search engine prominent in the middle of the one hundred and fifty-two centimeter screen. She looked up at Shakespeare, who smiled down at her, his chocolate brown eyes bright. She felt herself warming to this childhood toy of Bernie's, beginning to like the big guy. "Locate Min Bakster."

The search engine began to glow, then an address, contact link number, and picture of Min Bakster appeared. He didn't look as old as Shakespeare and Bernie had suggested.

Bakster couldn't be a day over a hundred and thirty-five. "A youngin'," she muttered under her breath.

Sheila turned her head to gaze at Bernie. "Old man? Really?"

Bernie shrugged sheepishly in response.

She chuckled. "Connect with the Bakster link," she said, turning her attention back to the screen.

There was a soft buzz, then the Min Bakster in the picture on his ID file appeared on the screen. Sheila actually thought he looked younger than the digital picture on file. Not surprising with all the regeneration techniques improving every day, it seemed.

Bakster was dressed in a mint-green, short-sleeved dress shirt, his steel gray hair cut short, his azure eyes alert, the corners slightly crinkled. He wore a half smile on his thin, pale lips.

"Yes? Can I help you?" he asked, obviously curious. His eyes briefly widened when his blue-green gaze shifted to the Bigfoot standing beside her, but he didn't seem all that startled by Shakespeare's appearance. Alien contact really had made everyone so blasé these days about seeing odd beings, which a few centuries ago would have brought out the military with guns a blazing.

Good thing, too, she thought. The early days of first contact had not been pretty.

"Hello, Min Bakster," she began, "I'm Sheila Culpepper, and this is Shakespeare. This is going to sound odd, but forty years ago my husband Bernie Culpepper and Shake—"

"Yes, I know who they are," Bakster said, interrupting her. His brow wrinkled in a frown and his eyes narrowed. His lips formed a grim line. "They caused me all sorts of trouble."

He looked as if he was about to cut the connection, but Sheila needed more information if they were going to solve this mystery. Bernie could be focused to the point of obsession.

Even after all these decades, no doubt this problem had been haunting him. Now, with the mystery rekindled, he would become impossible to live with.

"I'm sorry, Min Bakster, but I need to know if you recall another boy in the old neighborhood named Cruz."

His features became hard and his jawline tightened.

"Listen," she said, speaking softly. "I am really sorry if the boys upset you, but I really need to talk to this Cruz person."

Bakster's features relaxed slightly. Sheila knew she could charm even the most hardened curmudgeon; it appeared that included Bakster. *It's a gift.*

"Sorry if I'm being difficult, Sheila Culpepper, but Bernie and Shakespeare put up posters all over town saying I was missing." His features squished up as if he'd sucked on a sour lemon. "They described me as *old.* I've spent plenty on rejuvenation over the years just to be called *old*?" His scowl deepened. "It was humiliating."

Sheila wanted to laugh but managed to hold back by changing the subject. "Please call me Sheila....May I call you Min?" He nodded. "Okay, Min, if you tell me where Cruz is, I can clear all this up." She shifted her gaze to Bernie, whose face was red as beet soup. "And I'll make sure Bernie sends you a written apology for his youthful exuberance."

Bernie nodded sheepishly.

Min nodded. "Good, it's about time. You'll find Cruz..."

Sheila's heart began to beat rapidly when Min told them where to find Cruz. She looked up at Shakespeare, who had a wide grin on his furry face.

"Cool!" said Ryder.

***

Sheila stood beside Bernie, with Ryder holding her husband's hand. They stood in front of the viewing window overlooking the large, open launch area where six orbital shuttle pods were being prepared for liftoff. One ivory-white shuttle pod in particular had their attention.

Bernie's father was secured ion the stasis pod where Shakespeare had been kept for forty years. It would keep him alive until the doctors on Shakespear's woeld could save his life with their advanced medical knowledge.

The craft had twin antigravity engine exhausts extending from the rear of the passenger compartment. The short wings had been extended from the bottom of the craft, hiding the tripod landing skids, to aid in stability while the shuttle was still in the atmosphere. The two pilots were visible in windows of the command deck at the front of the pod, their attention focused on final checks before liftoff. Liftoff was set for ten minutes from now.

The shuttle pod would rendezvous with the deep space freighter headed for Shakespeare's races planet in less than an hour. Then the childhood toy Bernie had created would be gone. Though he was created on Earth he really wanted to visit the planet where his race originated. How could Bernie deny him?

"You okay?" Sheila asked, seeing the wistful expression on her husband's face.

"Yeah. I'm fine...I guess. I'm gonna miss him."

Sheila chuckled. "I know, but you haven't seen him in decades; and if what he says is true, he's going to save your father's life on his home world. Shakespeare's people know more about genetics than any race in the galaxy. They know how to save Dad's life.

110

"Given the distance to his world, I don't think you'll see Shakespeare again; but your dad will be back in fifty years or so."

Bernie turned to gaze into her eyes. "I owe this all to Bel Cruz. and Min of course. I'd say they're pretty good guys."

Ryder laughed. "Good thing Bel's a star pilot. He knew where Shakespeare's home planet is as soon as he saw him. Talk about a small world."

Bernie smiled. "No, son, it's a small galaxy."

Then they watched in silence as the shuttle pod carrying Shakespeare and Bernie's father lifted off. It began to grow gradually smaller and smaller until it was lost against the azure, cloudless sky.

Superheroes exist to stop super villains. It's a simple premise. A story told from the perspective of the henchman of the villain provides a different perspective than the usual superhero story.

Replacement Parts

Dr. Xavier Devlin is a misunderstood genius and my creator.

My name is Ambrose and I'm watching my creator in the damp, musty cave where Dr. Devlin is putting the final touches on his newest invention, a time machine.

I know you're thinking, Whhhhaaat?, but he really is a genius so if he says he's building a time machine then that is exactly what he's doing. I hope.

The doctor had made all of the screws and bolts and the steel walls for his machine using the forge in the next cave. The hint of coal smoke still hung in the air from the fire he built in the forge to soften and work the steel.

But events have not been going well for Dr. Devlin and I of late. In fact I felt useless to him as his assistant. What was my purpose if I couldn't help him in his work?

He was run out of San Francisco by his nemesis, Mr. Indestructible, a self-titled super hero with an enormous ego. Then the doctor's dog died. Kong was simply put the best wolf dog hybrid ever. He ripped apart so many of the doctor's enemies I've lost count. Then we were exiled to this dank system of twisting caves deep beneath the Cascade mountain range to our current lair.

Mr. Indestructible discovered all our previous lairs before the doctor made much headway on his plans to take over the world. Also Mr. Indestructible destroyed the wave-making machine Dr. Devlin planned to use to clear the California coast so his Utopian city could be constructed. The future of mankind needed Dr. Devlin; they just didn't appreciate him yet.

The damp cave we were using at our latest lair assaulted my nose and mouth with the biting odor of rotting mold. Dr. Devlin had made my senses keener than the average human so I was especially sensitive to this environment.

I sneezed when the sandy floor trembled beneath my feet and a cloud of dust from the cave roof overhead filled the room with grit invading my nose and mouth. That pesky so-called hero was no doubt tunneling in from the surface in an attempt to stop Dr. Devlin from completing his latest invention. Gifted with the strength of ten locomotives meant Mr. Indestructible is capable of tunneling through solid rock as simple as slicing through sun-warmed cheese. I expected he'd be here soon; time was likely growing short for our escape.

"Ambrose, hand me the wrench," Dr. Devlin said with his back turned to me.

I stood next to the wooden workbench loaded with hammer's screws, nails, and wrenches still coughing from the dust shower. When I didn't react immediately his request Dr. Devlin spun round to face me. His intense dark eyes locked on mine and a single thin, black eyebrow arched on his pale forehead. His angular features and narrow bloodless lips paired with his glare causing me to freeze where I stood. The dark goggles he wore were perched above his forehead pressed into his shoulder length ink black hair.

Dr. Devlin wiped his grease stained hands on his apron. "Ambrose, I asked for the wrench. I need to tighten these bolts on the side of the machine." He nodded to the large steel bolts running down both sides of the machine that looked like a booth in some magic show at the carnival.

Like all of his inventions this one was steam powered and constructed from steel and tempered glass. Unlike his other inventions this one seemed oddly out of place. A working time machine seemed a bit of a stretch even for a genius.

Unfortunately, I was frozen by fear my gusts twisting my heart pounding hard against my ribs. "Huh, sir...doctor..."

The doctor's features morphed into a wide smile. "Let's take a break. I need a coffee."

Thinking it unwise to delay but always obedient to the doctor's wishes, I nodded then followed Dr. Devlin to the living quarters located off the cave where he worked. The quarters were spartan with a cot where he slept, a pine table and two matching chairs one on either side, a small fire pit under a natural stone vent, and an oil lamp. Against one wall was a supply cupboard. Stacked next to the cot rose a stack of books on every subject from growing vegetables to Greek history, and from biology to physics. The odd thing about these books is the copyright dates are a hundred years in the future.

When I asked him Dr. Devlin explained these dates were printing errors. But in the book?

Dr. Devlin went to retrieve the coffee pot off the table and placed it next to the still glowing embers of the fire in the pit. No doubt it would be strong when it came up to temperature but he seemed to enjoy strong coffee.

He sat at the table while I sat across from him on the other chair.

He sighed heavily and removed the tinted goggles setting them on the table next to where he'd placed his mug of steam fragrant coffee. Using two fingers of his right hand he pinched his hawk-like nose between them, closed his eyes, and begin to rub both sides of his nose. With his wide shoulders slumped slightly forward he looked tired and older than I had ever seen him. For the first time in a long time I wondered how old he really was.

"Huh, doctor, may I ask a personal question?"

He stopped rubbing his eyes and regarded me his features impassive and his inky eyes free of emotion. "Of course, Ambrose, ask away." Dr. Devlin eased against the back of the chair and crossed one leg over the other his hands now folded in his lap.

A knot of worry formed in my guts. Maybe I was being too forward?

"Hummm...doctor, I am puzzled about something."

One corner of Dr. Devlin's mouth curled slightly up and his eyes flashed. He sipped at his coffee. "Yes, Ambrose?"

"Well, you see the books you read...their copyright dates are strange...and sometimes you use unfamiliar words..." My words trailed off as Dr. Devlin's eyes sparkled with undisguised humor. The doctor sometimes used words like computer, and cell phone, texting, Internet, and others. In the nineteen century such words have no meaning, which meant the doctor had to be from somewhere....no, sometime else.

"So what conclusion have you come to?" The doctor stood tossed the remaining coffee in his cup onto floor then walked to coffee pot next to the fire and poured himself another cup.

A deep rumble from somewhere overhead made me pause before I spoke. The floor trembled under foot briefly then once again settled.

"I think this time machine you're building isn't the first one you've built. I believe you are a time traveler." I finished feeling suddenly confident having finally aired my inner thoughts.

Dr. Devlin regarded me his eyes thoughtful for several seconds then he sat at the table once again and set the steel mug on the table. "Actually you are correct, my dear Ambrose, more correct than you know actually." He sighed as he leaned back in the chair, which creaked softly in the silence.

Dr. Devlin began to relate his tale.

"I began my experiments in the year 2123. At first I created one man using genetic modification of a human genome." He took a sip of coffee swallowed then continued. I created several more until I had six in total, including one female.

"They were faster, more intelligent, stronger, than any humans in history. My goal was to create a race of supermen to rid the world of war, disease, poverty, and terrorism.

"Unfortunately, much like the fictional Dr. Frankenstein my creations turned on me and instead of adhering to the path I had set for them they became super heroes bent on stopping my plans to re-invent a corrupt world."

The room shook violently for several seconds as we were showered in dust and debris from the cave roof. The coffee pot beside the fire fell over and a pool of hot coffee formed at the edge of the fire dousing some of the flames like some ravenous beast as it spread. One of the oil lamps hung off steel hooks I'd embedded in the cave wall fell to the sand covered floor.

Fortunately the oil tank didn't shatter but the cloud of dust it created snuffed out the flame.

Looking down I saw my hands were gripping opposite sides of the table my knuckles had drained of color. My heart pounded in my chest and my mouth was free of any trace of moisture. The doctor sat across from me his eyes watchful with a slight grin on his lips.

"Did you feel that?" I said my voice trembling with fear.

Dr. Devlin nodded. "Oh, yes, indeed I did. Mr. Indestructible will be here sooner than my original calculations predicted." He pulled a pocket watch from his pants pocket and flipped it open. "Quite remarkable actually. This mountain has a combination of ores that should have slowed him down."

"How can you be so calm, doctor? Mr. Indestructible is going to be here within seconds."

The doctor's only response was to smile and nod. He locked his gaze on the coffee mug as one wall of the cave exploded inward causing a small avalanche of rock and dust quickly obscuring my view of not only my immediate surroundings but also the doctor who was enveloped by a cloud.

Coughing, choking, and waving my arms I stood and stumbled to where I hoped was the cavern containing the time machine. Knowing Dr. Devlin as well as I had come to over the years we'd worked together I knew he'd be able to find his way without my help.

As I managed to find the entrance to adjacent cave where the dust wasn't as bad. Through the choking haze, my eyes watering I spotted the time machine and a man-shaped figure standing next to the device. It was Dr. Devlin busy using the wrench to tighten the bolts.

He finished as I approached dropping the wrench in the dirt where it landed with a sharp bang off a rock. Dr. Devlin turned to face me his expression dark and serious his eyes narrow. I'm familar with this expression. He was focused on a plan.

I opened my mouth to speak but a loud grinding sound of a wall collapsing opposite of where we stood interrupted me.

Mr. Indestructible stepped through the space vacated by the collapse of the wall and calmly stared at us. His blond curly hair neatly swept back from his wide forehead, calm bright blue eyes the color of summer sun on pond water stood with his hands on his hips. He wore the familar forest green one-piece jumpsuit and the brown leather gloves and boots to finish off his super hero persona.

I've always thought he looked ridiculous but the women seemed to think he was handsome. Or at least the articles in the newspapers said women swooned over him. Personally I don't see it but then I'm not fond of men with giant egos.

"Ah," said Indestructible, "Dr. Xavier Devlin and his lackey, Ambrose. At last I capture you both."

Dr. Devlin smirked adding a grunt of derision. He crossed his arms over his chest and glared at his nemesis. I had a front row seat to watch this confrontation of the titans of science and the opposite ends of good versus evil. Dr. Devlin is of course the good side of that equation. He only wants the best for human kind. Indestructible is all about positive press. He could care less who gets hurt by his actions.

On the other hand the doctor sacrificed the few to advance the best of humanity. He regretted these actions but knew this corrupt world needed his intervention. And I agree.

The doctor shook his head. "I don't think you've captured anyone, Milton."

Mr. Indestructible dropped his arms to his sides and his smooth forehead wrinkled as his confident grin faded from his features. "As you very well know, Dr. X, I detest that name."

"And you know I don't appreciate the name Dr. X," retaliated Dr. Devlin.

Indestructible grunted and raised his gloved hands in mock surrender. "I know, doctor, I apologize, but the name you gave me when you created me garners bad memories for me and it makes me hostile."

Dr. Devlin walked to stand a couple of feet away from Indestructible apparently willing to confront the so-called hero who had strength far surpassing his own and who could snap him as if he were a twig.

My knees became like lemon gelatin and I wondered if I should retreat to the other cave to bring back a chair to sit on and watch this argument between foes. I decided to stay where I stood, at least for now.

Dr. Devlin snorted. "Every time I see you all we discuss is how badly I raised you. When will you let it go?"

Indestructible walked to stand next to me then raised one gloved finger to point at me. "Ambrose doesn't look anything like me. " He placed one muscular arm across my narrow shoulders.

His arm was unbelievably heavy as if it were made of lead. I had to struggle to stay standing.

"Of course he doesn't," Dr. Devlin's features flushed crimson and his eyes blazed with anger. "He's for replacement part—" Dr. Devlin cut himself off his eyes wide his mouth hanging open. "I...I mean I perfected Ambrose after you and your brothers and your sister betrayed me. I needed a loyal assistant in order to complete my mission."

It was as if a pile of bricks had suddenly landed on me knocking out my breath. My skin became cool and damp as a knot of anger began to form in my belly. I shrugged Mr. Indestructible's arm off my shoulder. "Dr. Devlin, what did you mean when you said I'm for replacement parts?" My hands formed fists at my sides.

The doctor eyes sagged at the corners. "I'm sorry you had to find out this way, Ambrose." He paused and I saw him swallow before he continued. "I needed a way to create replacement parts for my creations should they need them. You and Milt are a genetic match, you literally are genetic twins."

Indestructible snorted derisively. "Me and this...this weakling?"

I stepped forward to within inches of the so-called super heroes face and pointed one index finger with a fraction of an inch of his nose. Mr. Indestructible was startled and took a half step backward his eyes wide. I suspect I was the only still living person to have ever challenged his personal space in such a bold manner. I detected the scent of whiskey on his breath I was so close.

Heroes drink spirits? I thought they were supposed to be pure and unspoiled by human vices. I shook off this distraction; there were other matters to be dealt with.

"You watch your tongue you phony excuse for a hero. You're no better than me and I'd have to be dead before you ever got any of my parts."

It dawned on me immediately I may have uttered a verbal faux pas that could be misconstrued as a sexual innuendo Dr. Devlin had cautioned me about double meanings of words during our numerous discussions about modern human failings and his plans to build a better world through re-engineering. Sexual innuendo was at the top of the list.

Clear communications were critical to my eventually becoming human.

Sure enough Mr. Indestructible eye's flitted to Dr. Devlin then back to me. A small smile crossed his lips. Darn it. I had lessened the meaning of my threat. Fortunately Dr. Devlin intervened to save my self-respect.

"Milt, never mind all this, Ambrose isn't going anywhere with you anyway and besides in the next 45 seconds this cave will collapse in on all us burying my dream, but also locking you away from the world."

Mr. Indestructible stared at Dr. Devlin seemingly unable to speak, his expression a mix of fear, anger, and doubt. He must have realized, as did I, if this imminent destruction were true this lair, the time machine, the assertion that I was a replacement for Mr. Indestructible, was a trap to destroy this windbag egomaniac of a super hero. Dr. Devlin would finally triumph over his nemesis at the expense of his own life.

Mr. Indestructible seemed to recover from the initial shock. His back straightened as he flexed the muscles in his arms. His brow wrinkled and he glared at the doctor his lips formed a grim line and his eyes locked on Dr. Devlin's who looked impassive as if he didn't care we all about to die.

"Doctor, I don't believe you." Mr. Indestructible's hands formed fists and his thick muscular frame tensed, his muscles seemingly about to burst through his uniform.

Dr. Devlin shrugged. "Believe what you want." He extracted his silver pocket watch and it flipped open. He looked at the clock face then closed it and slipped back in his pocket. "We're just about out of time."

Mr. Indestructible turned to address me. "Ambrose, you and I are brothers, please tell me, was Dr. Devlin working on anything in this lair?"

My eyes flitted to the doctor who appeared unfazed apparently willing to do nothing before the mountain crashed down on us. Rather than saying anything my eyes then flitted to the time machine standing undamaged across the cave.

Mr. Indestructible followed my gaze his blue eyes landing on the machine. A grin spread brightened his features. "Ahhhh, a teleporter I assume?"

I nodded nervously.

"Good." Mr. Indestructible rushed to the machine. Throwing open the door he stepped inside. Before he closed the door he warned us not to try to stop him or follow him. "Farewell, Dr. X, and his moronic assistant."

Indestructible slapped his open palm on the button on the control surface. The machine began to glow brighter and brighter until I was forced to look away. Finally heated air washed over the machine and my sight obscured by a cloud of steam. My nostrils were filled with the smell of super heated water, it had a musty scent.

"Well, Ambrose, now we can get back to work without interference."

I looked at Dr. Devlin aghast. "But I thought...I mean you said..."

Dr. Devlin smirked. "Just because I made him indestructible doesn't mean I made him intelligent. He walked into and activated my trap. He's gone now."

"You tricked him?"

Dr. Devlin smiled and walked to stand beside me curling one long arm around my shoulder and pulled me close him.

"You and I have a few things to talk about. Before we were so rudely interrupted I was going to explain more about us."

"Where did he go?" I said nodding toward the dissipating cloud of steam.

Dr. Devlin shrugged. "I have no idea. The machine is a time machine, but Milt could be anywhere in any time. I didn't have time to calibrate the controls." He led me toward the other cave. "But I want you to clean up this mess so we can get started on my next project."

"Which is what, sir?"

Dr. Devlin stopped walking and a wistful expression crossed his features. He released my shoulder in order to face me. "Milt gave me an excellent idea when he barged in here. I think I'll construct an earthquake machine and hold the world's government hostage until they pay enormous ransoms." He grinned. "What do you think?"

"Honestly? I think it needs work, doctor."

Dr. Devlin laughed. "Yes, of course it does. Oh, and you may call me Xavier from now on, Ambrose."

I shook my head. "No, sorry, doctor I can't do that."

Dr. Devlin smiled and nodded. "I understand."

We entered the part of the cave used as the doctors living quarters and saw there was a considerable mess to clean up. The self-titled Mr. Indestructible had created a lot of destruction.

But I was encouraged, in fact my guts bubbled with excitement. The future looked bright and I would be part of a new Utopia created by the most brilliant scientist in the world.

My purpose in the orbit of a genius finally made sense to me. I wasn't just replacement parts to him. I was his creation and he saved me.

This odd little story came from an old pulp magazine title. Where it landed was a question? What ever happened to all the jugglers, plate twirlers, acrobats and others acts that appeared on the old Ed Sullivan Show?

Mind Readers

PETER "PUMPKIN" JONES' WATCH COMMANDER, Assistant Superintendant Ian Serious, burst through the glass entrance doors of the Vancouver Police headquarters, a man on a mission. His azure eyes blazed with anger and his muscular arms appeared ready to burst through his white uniform dress shirt. Pumpkin had the sinking feeling his boss' bad mood involved him and his partner, Arnie "Slant" Slantosky. They'd been his favorite targets since they were assigned to the Super's watch six months ago.

"Jones." Serious growled his name as if he were chewing glass. "I want you and Slantosky in my office. Now."

The lieutenant disappeared through the Staff Only door on the right side of the public reception lobby, the door slamming shut behind him.

Pumpkin sighed as he rose from the chair he'd been sitting in behind the desk. The wall separated reception from the open office where the officers coming off shift completed their reports.

The reception counter was separated by a wall of bullet proof glass from people coming in off the street to file reports for missing dogs, lost keys, misplaced musical instruments, or to ask inane questions. During each shift all he seemed to do was answer questions like; "How long does it take to drive to Winnipeg?" or "What's the weather report for Costa Rica today?"

(The answers of course are, "As long as it takes." and "Too damned hot and too damned humid.")

Pumpkin had been stuck behind this desk for the past three months and it was driving him nuts. I'm a cop damn it, not a Post-it note.

When would the Super forgive and forget his little accident? Sure, totaling the mayor's car seemed bad but the brakes on the cruiser had seemed to fail (though the fleet mechanic said the limo's brakes were in perfect condition) and the street was slick with rain, so how could the accident be completely his fault? He accepted fifty percent of the blame; the rest was an act of God.

Yes, Slant and he had been playing a spirited game of I-spy-with-my-little-eye so his attention wasn't completely on the road, but how was being young and free suddenly a bad thing? These stuff shirts didn't appreciate his skills.

And why did the mayor's driver park his car in the no loading zone? I should have issued him a ticket instead of requesting a tow truck, muttered Pumpkin under his breath.

"Another officer will be here in a minute," he called out to the reception waiting area filled with raggedy ass people, drug addicts, and an assortment of unknown species of inner city wild life each holding a slip of paper with a number on it from the never ending flotsam of humanity.

After summoning a replacement officer he exited the reception area through the door at the rear of the long, narrow room. It's like being a monkey in a glass cage.

He walked to stand beside Slant's desk at the rear of a row of six identical metal desks each with a computer terminal in one corner. His partner's job was to read on-line newspapers from across the country, and the U.S., looking for items of interest to the watch commanders. Serious had given him a list of key words submitted by the four watch commanders.

His job was to identify the stories, print them off, and then clip them together for the day. He would then place the day's batch of stories into a basket at one corner of his desk for pickup by the watch commanders when they came on duty.

The out-basket currently struggled to contain a leaning tower of paper so high that from certain angles, Slant, who was a plus sized man over six feet in height, disappeared completely. Pumpkin concluded this was the Super's point behind this make-work project.

The Super would have fired them both if he could, but the Police Association, and the Chief Super wouldn't let him. This pissed the Super off so much he became even harder on them, but Pumpkin and Slant weren't quitters.

Five years slaving away in the City Works Department as Sewer Technicians, before passing the Police Academy entrance exam, made them tough and uncompromising. Of course riding around in a shiny patrol car was certainly preferable to cleaning sewer pipes all day, and you smelled of donuts and coffee instead of toilet water, which was certainly a bonus.

"Hey, partner, how goes the battle?" he asked after watching Slant for several seconds squinting at the computer screen in front of him.

The computer was the only dial up model left on the force so it shrieked loudly every time he connected to the Internet. The dial up connection meant the download times were so slow it would have been faster to run to the newsstand on Granville Street that carried newspapers from across the country and read them all than wait for even one screen to populate.

Slant eased back in the ergonomic chair and rubbed his eyes with the palms of both hands. "Man, I'm going blind and stir crazy simultaneously." Dropping his hands away from his eyes he peered up at Pumpkin. His red-rimmed eyes gave Pumpkin a start. "When are we getting back on the road?" Slant's eyes pleaded with him.

For the first time in the past three months Pumpkin worried Slant might throw in the towel and submit his resignation. Wouldn't the Super love that?

Before speaking Pumpkin recalled the line from his favorite movie, "Fly casual." His pal needed him to be calm right now. He chuckled easily. "Today might be the day, 'ol buddy."

Slant's watery, hazel eyes opened wide and he shifted his butt forward on the chair. "What do you mean?" He raised his voice causing the officers seated at the desks nearby to look in their direction.

Pumpkin grabbed an empty chair from the desk next to Slant's and sat down. He lowered his voice to a whisper and placed one hand on his friend's arm. "Lower your voice, bud." Slant nodded but his pale complexion was now the color of red beets.

He's losing it; I hope the Super's news is good.

"The Super wants to see us in his office right away."

"Really? We're finally going to get out of here?"

"I'd be willing to bet that hand," Pumpkin said, bluffing just like he did at their monthly poker game. Fortunately, Slant fell for his bluffs every time.

Pumpkin stood as Slant bounced to his feet. His friend reminded him of a puppy who'd just been given a fresh bone.

They soon stood in front of the Assistant Superintendent's desk in his office listening to the Super chew out Sergeant Tums on his cell phone.

Pumpkin squinted at the wall behind the Super's desk and discovered his boss had received another honorary award to add to his collection of meaningless plaques and phony awards covering nearly every square inch of the wall from the ceiling to the floor. Anymore phony awards and he'd need a new wall or, as Pumpkin was sure Serious dreamt of every night, a promotion with a larger office.

The Men Supporting Opera Society bestowed this latest cheaply framed treasure on the Super. Pumpkin had to stop himself from smirking. He didn't need to be on Serious' only remaining worse side, he'd already maxed out the Super's worst side quotient for this lifetime.

Finally, Serious finished the call then tossed his cell phone on top of a short stack of papers on his desk. He glowered in silence at them his eyes flicking between them.

Pumpkin felt Slant tremble under the Super's stare. Pumpkin wanted to jump over the desk and rip out Serious' throat for torturing her fragile friend, but murdering the boss stunted a career path so he restrained himself.

"I really hate you guys," Serious growled. He looked away and shook his head slowly. "But the chief wants you both for a special assignment." He spat the words as if they were sour milk.

"Yes, sir," said Pumpkin.

Serious' eyes shot to glare at Pumpkin. "Pumpkin Jones is no name for a cop, a purveyor of fine farm produce maybe, but not a bonafide cop."

The Super stood up behind his desk causing Pumpkin and Slant to take a step backward fearing the boss might hit them, shoot them, or something equally bad. "But screw that," Serious continued, "it's not important right now. You two morons are to report to Sergeant Tums at the water treatment plant in False Creek."

The water treatment plant? The water treatment plant was the end of the long lonesome piss trail, as they referred to the place when they were sewer techs.

"Uhhh, sir, why?" asked Pumpkin. He stole a glance at Slant and saw he looked pleased to be leaving the office. Not that he blamed his friend but this assignment sounded fishy. Or maybe salty was the better word?

"Did I say you could ask questions?" Serious glared at them.

"Uhhh, no, sir. Sorry. Sir."

"Then get the hell out of my office. I told Sergeant Tums to call me when you're done."

Once outside the Super's office Slant looked like a kid on the last day of school before Christmas holidays. "We're outta here!" He ran away leaving Pumpkin standing amongst the desks filled by officers arriving for work or preparing to leave for the day. Since it was shift change the room was full of people and all eyes were at him.

"Sorry, guys and gals, he's a little excited about a top secret mission for the chief." Grinning sheepishly he held both hands up palms open. "Before you ask modesty prevents me from providing the details. Let's just say we'll be seeing you all at the medal ceremony."

Bill Parker, who stood to his left leaning against a filing cabinet with his arms crossed over his chest, laughed then in a mocking tone said, "I hear you guys are assigned to the water treatment plant. You rejoining the sewer patrol?"

The assembled officers laughed as Pumpkin hurriedly left the room through a side door to join Slant in the locker room. His face felt warm and his heart beat rapidly.

I'll show them. We'll get those medals and be heroes, or my name isn't Pumpkin Jones.

***

Standing ankle deep in dirty water Pumpkin played the beam of his flashlight over the tunnel walls. The curved surfaces were coated with green slime and dark brown water ran in small rivulets from random patches of coal black moss growing on the surface of the riveted steel plates used to build the tunnel walls.

Slant used his flashlight looking for eels or snakes that might be lurking in the murky water. Pumpkin assured his partner there was no chance such creatures could possibly survive in the contaminated water.

The bright yellow environmental suits, complete with hoods, breathing tanks and heavy, insulated boots, protected them from not only any contaminants in the water, or on the surface of the curved tunnel of steel, but also the air, which no doubt reeked of toxic chemicals. The suit helmets muffled their voices but they could still hear each other through the Plexiglas faceplate.

Constructed in 1899 the original wastewater tunnel system had mostly remained untouched for over a hundred years. It was very likely they were the first humans that ever ventured this deep into these tunnels since they were constructed.

The farther they went into the maze of tunnels the more Pumpkin's dreams of medals and accolades began to fade.

Sergeant Tums told them two treatment plant technicians had gone into the tunnels and hadn't been seen for three days.

The chief requested Pumpkin and Slant conduct the search for the missing technicians specifically because of their experience in the sanitation department. And because the chief believed in them, or so Tums said before ordering them into the tunnels. Pumpkin suspected the rest of the sanitation staff had refused to enter these uncharted waters to look for their staff, and no doubt their union supported their decision.

Caught between the choice of quitting the police force, or doing the job, what choice did they have? Much like Dorothy, the Scarecrow, the Cowardly Lion, and the Tin Man they set off into the tunnels looking for the missing technicians. Too bad the road's made of slimy, dark brown water instead of yellow bricks.

After two hours of slogging through the murky water Pumpkin suggested they rest for a few minutes before continuing. Slant agreed and they stopped at a junction where the pipe divided into two tunnels each running in opposite directions. Pumpkin had hoped there were maps of the tunnels, but the original maps had been destroyed in a fire over sixty years ago

Breathing hard, Slant rested his back against the tunnel wall with his eyes closed while Pumpkin scanned the two tunnels alternating the flashlight beam between them trying to decide which tunnel they should go into next. Pumpkin considered flipping a coin only the insulated suit covered his pants pockets and he wasn't about to take it off or remove his helmet. If they had straws they could each draw one to decide, but the fact straw didn't grow in the dark nixed the idea, and there were no fast food joints nearby to get some plastic ones.

He directed the beam over the waterproof watch on his left wrist and saw they had six hours of air remaining which meant they had to turn back in another two hours or they'd run out of air before they got back to the plant.

Pumpkin didn't like the idea of failing, but so far they hadn't discovered any clues to the whereabouts of the missing technicians.

Something floating in the water at the edge of the beam of yellow light cast by the flashlight caught his eye in one of the tunnels. Stepping closer to get a better look he was shocked to discover a large wooden puppet, or more properly, a ventriloquist's dummy, floating in the water. It looked like a caricature of a man, with short brown hair, cut pageboy style, a red and blue plaid shirt, and red suspenders. The dummies stubby legs were covered by black pants and on its tiny feet were white canvass running shoes.

The expression on the puppet's chubby cheeked features took him aback. The black pupiless eyes were beady, the skin the color of red beets, the mouth was shaped in a sneer. It didn't look anything like the friendly puppets he'd seen on television growing up. In fact it looked kind of evil.

The only good thing about finding the dummy was it was their first clue. "Hey, Slant, look what I found." He picked the puppet up by one arm and lifted it from the water. Slant sighed wearily and opened his eyes. Gazing upon the dripping puppet his eyes grew wide. "Is that a ventriloquists dummy?"

Pumpkin chuckled. "Yup, I found it in this tunnel." He nodded his head slightly toward the tunnel to the right.

Slant stepped away from the wall and joined Pumpkin in looking over the strange doll. Gripping the dummy in one gloved hand Pumpkin turned it over and discovered a clear plastic bag with a price of white paper inside pinned to the puppet's back.

Glancing at Slant, who seemed eager to investigate, he pulled the pin out releasing the bag, which he handed to Slant. The bag was a food storage bag so it had a resalable strip along one edge. Undoing the strip Slant pulled the piece of paper from the bag revealing handwriting.

Unfolding it he held his flashlight beam over the writing. "Hey, this is like one of them notes in a bottle," he said. His brow wrinkled as he read the note. "It's written by someone named Helen Pinky who says she's being held against her will by what she calls the mind readers of the tunnels. She wants to be rescued."

"Does it say where she's being held?"

Slant turned the document over. "Uhhh, no. Too bad. We'd get medals for sure if we rescued her."

"You know what this means don't you?" asked Pumpkin. Slant looked at him his expression registering his confusion. Pumpkin grinned. "It means this is a job for Pumpkin and Slant, hero cops of the VPD."

***

Pumpkin lead the way through to the tunnel where he'd found the floating ventriloquists dummy hoping it would lead to the woman who wrote the note. As they walked the level of the water went lower and lower until when they arrived at a steel door blocking further progress, the water had disappeared completely. The steel grating on the floor was dry and free of moss.

The door had no handle so Pumpkin felt around the seams where the door was attached to the frame. Unfortunately there didn't appear to be a way to open it. Glancing at his watch he realized they had to turn back in thirty minutes anyway.

"Let's go back. I'll file a report with the Super and he can dispatch a search team with tools to take down this door." Pumpkin said, after giving up on finding any hidden latch or spring.

"Stay where you are." A man's husky voice that seemed familiar yet he couldn't quite place it, echoed off the steel walls.

Pumpkin and Slant swung their flashlights around them trying to find who had spoken, but there was no one there.

"Uhhh, can we help you?" asked Pumpkin his heart rate increasing. Before they entered the tunnels he considered bringing his gun, but since it would be hidden beneath the suit, and he couldn't reach it, he decided to leave his weapon with Sergeant Tums. Now he regretted that decision. He knew Slant always carried a hidden weapon, he hoped.

"Step back from the door," said the voice.

Slant looked to Pumpkin who nodded. They might as well do as the voice says since Pumpkin hadn't found a way in. He hoped they'd find Helen Pinky beyond the door.

A screech of metal on metal made Pumpkin wince as the door swung inward away from them. Bight light shone through the now open doorway forcing them to look away.

"Are you carrying any weapons?" said a woman's high-pitched voice.

Blinking his eyes rapidly, until they adjusted to the sudden burst of light Pumpkin could make out a fuzzy outline of a woman framed by doorway.

"Uhhh, no, we're not," Pumpkin said.

"Good. Please step through the door and follow me."

Slant went first followed by Pumpkin then the door closed behind them with a loud clang. They were trapped.

Pumpkin froze and sucked in a breath when his vision had cleared completely. For a second he thought his mind was tricking him, but what he saw was real.

They were standing on a grassy hilltop looking over a vast city of spires, glass towers that disappeared into the curve of the horizon. A network of streets in a checkerboard patter ran left and right in between the buildings. The streets were busy with three-wheeled egg shaped vehicles moving about like ants. The buildings and spires rose a hundred feet into the air, sparkled and glowed under light pouring down from above.

Shielding his eyes with one hand he looked up and saw a hundreds of banks of light bars, some six feet wide, while others were smaller. His eyes began to water under the assault of the lights so Pumpkin looked away.

"We have the lights on day time setting. You should see the city at night."

Pumpkin looked at the woman startled to discover she was a small person who had the bluest, most piercing eyes he had ever seen. Her irises were like two pools of lake water on a sunny day.

"Where are we?" he said.

"This is the Parish of Talent, or POT for short."

"OK, but really, where are we?"

The woman chuckled. "Hi, I'm Helen Pinky." She offered her right hand in greeting. She had on a one piece tanned jumpsuit with the name Pinky stitched in red thread over the left breast. Her straight hair, a brassy reddish color, was cut shoulder length parted to one side.

Bending from the waist Pumpkin took her small hand in his. Her skin was warm and soft to the touch. He released her hand and stood up right. "Hi, Helen, if I may call you Helen..." she nodded, "I'm Peter Jones, this is my partner..." He nodded at Slant.

138

"Arnie Slantosky."

Her eyes were warm, her easy grin friendly. If Helen was the welcome wagon then she was the perfect hostess for the job.

"Of course, Officer Jones" she nodded at him then at Slant. "And Officer Slantosky...or may I call you, Pumpkin and Slant?"

Pumpkins heart skipped a beat. She knew who they were, even their nicknames. If he'd met a little person who looked like Helen before he would have remembered. Then again..."Have we met?"

"Oh, my, no. The mind readers knew you were coming to the parish before you did."

"Mind readers?"

"Yes," she said, her china doll features brightening as she warmed to the topic. "We knew after the two sanitation workers stumbled upon our community others would be dispatched to look for them. The mind readers began to probe beyond our borders and soon discovered Assistant Superintendent Serious assigned you and Slant to search the tunnels."

She walked away toward a three-wheeled vehicle like the ones on the streets far below the hill. It too was oval in shape and fire engine red. "You can take off those suits, you won't need them while you're in the POT."

Pumpkin looked at Slant who shook his head, his friend's eyes were wide with what Pumpkin knew to be fear. Helen wasn't wearing an environmental suit and she seemed normal, normal being defined somewhat liberally given the situation, so he decided it was worth the risk to do what she said, at least for now. Besides, she could have killed them when the light blinded them if that was her agenda. In his experience everyone had an agenda, and hers intrigued him, he needed to know more.

"Com'on, Slant, let's go along with her for now. OK?" Pumpkin knew Slant trusted his judgment so after he nodded Slant removed his helmet. After sucking in a deep breath, and not collapsing, Pumpkin did likewise.

Once they had the protective suits off they folded them and left them on the grass near the door. Helen was waiting for them in the car. Before joining Helen in the car, Pumpkin checked the air gauge in the suit tanks. There would be ten minutes of air to spare if they had to make a break for it through the tunnels.

This mind reader bit she talked about had to be crap. There must be another way to the surface from this city. Then again he had never heard of this underground city, not even a rumor such a place existed. How could a city this large exist without anyone knowing?

Now dressed in his navy blue police issue cargo pants and cotton shirt, Pumpkin rode next to Helen in the front passenger seat while Slant, also in uniform, sat in the back.

The electric car lurched as Helen pressed a large stainless steel foot shaped pedal on the floor. It shot away quickly gaining speed on the two-lane ribbon cut between grassy hills similar to the one they'd just left.

"The Parish is divided into zones so each act can live with their kind." Helen explained as she drove. The drivers seat had inflated so she could see over the dashboard and the go and stop pedals rose from the floor so she could reach them with her booted feet.

(The words stop and go were etched into the stainless steel pedals in black capital letters.)

"Their kind?" Slant asked from the back seat.

Helen chuckled lightly. "It's not what you think. We're all performers specializing in certain types of acts; jugglers, plate twirlers, fire eaters, and mind readers to name a few.

"I'm part of a troupe of tumblers known as the Incredible Pinky Sisters. The residents here like to live with other performers of their particular talent to share ideas and reminisce about the good old days." She paused and he sensed something troubled her.

"Anyway, the POT is divided into sectors, you would call them neighborhoods, where each talent has access to a theater to practice their craft for the once a year Grand Showcase Gala at the Parish Central Theatre. The winners of each category are awarded eternal life."

"Eternal life? You people live forever?" Pumpkin was beginning to think these people were nuts. An underground society of people who live in groups of novelty acts? Crazy.

They'd left the rolling hills and entered a busy street of similar cars. Pumpkin started slack jawed at the people walking on the sidewalks.

Men and women twirled plates on long flexible poles, acrobats leapfrogged over each other, there was a man who looked like an African explorer, complete with pith helmet, held the hand of a monkey and several men dressed in white tie and tails with elaborate turbans covering their heads made Pumpkin swallow hard. They looked like mind reading acts from the old variety show days.

Helen was telling the truth at least about the residents of this underground city. He'd heard

Helen steered the car into traffic and picked up speed. "Not everyone, only the winners of the Gala."

"How many years have there been galas?" asked Slant.

"Fifty two."

"And how many winners?"

"Four thousand five hundred and six." Suddenly Helen jerked the car to the right and stopped beside the curb.

The car stopped so abruptly Pumpkin's seatbelt dug into his shoulder and chest. Pumpkin winced and Slant cried out in pain.

"Sorry, about that, I nearly missed the office I was talking so much."

Pumpkin rolled his shoulder trying to lessen the pain and vowed never to talk with Helen when she was driving. "No problem, Helen, at least we arrive safely." He gazed at the tall building they were parked in front of. "What's this building?"

Helen smiled as she slipped off her seat belt. "The Grand Mind Reader wishes to meet you. He has an offer for you."

One we can't refuse? Wondered Pumpkin.

***

Helen led the way into an office at the very top of the building. The floor to ceiling windows making up one wall overlooked the city spread across the skyline from one side to the other. The spectacular sight momentarily took away Pumpkins breath.

"Impressive isn't it?" Pumpkin recognized the man's gravelly voice coming from his right.

Looking toward the voice he froze and his heart began to beat rapidly. "Chief?" His mouth dried and his hands began to tremble.

VPD Chief Superintendent Buddy Mockton strode across the carpeted office wearing in his formal dress police uniform. He wore a lopsided grin on his angular features and his chocolate brown eyes sparkled with mirth. He held a glass in one hand with what Pumpkin assumed was whiskey and a couple of ice cubes.

"If it isn't old Slant and Pumpkin, or is it Pumpkin and Slant?"

"Yes, sir, it's good to see you too. Sir."

"Drink?" Mockton said raising his glass before taking a sip.

"No, sir. Thank you, sir." From the corner of one eye Pumpkin saw Slant open his mouth to speak. Pumpkin turned to glare at his partner until he too declined the offer. There'd be no drinking. He sensed they needed their wits about them if they wanted to get out of here alive. The chief's presence here meant he was right about their being another way to the surface. The chief wouldn't have come through the tunnels.

"So, sir, what gives with this place? Are you going to harvested our sperm, or perhaps serve us as the main course at dinner?"

The chief looked at Helen who had joined him behind his desk the cityscape filling the sky expansive windows. They suddenly burst our laughing.

Pumpkin looked at Slant who shrugged. "Sorry, sir, did I say something funny?"

The chief soon stopped laughing then sat down behind the desk in a brown leather executive chair. "Pumpkin, we don't eat people here or harvest their sperm. We're performers, novelty acts long forgotten by mainstream entertainment."

The chief eased back in his chair while Helen jumped up to sit on one corner of his desk. She was certainly agile. "You can learn an act and join us, like those two sanitation workers decided to do, or you can leave. It's really that simple."

"What about the ventriloquists dummy with the note pinned to its back?" blurted Slant.

The chief snorted and his eyes flicked to Helen then shifted to Slant. "Slantosky, you don't get it do you?" Slant shook his head. "It's true our population is dwindling and we do need fresh blood to keep our society thriving. Without a stable population our acts will die out completely from the cultural consciousness forever. Oh, we send invitations to people venturing into the tunnels.

In your case you're cops. Well, in the case of you two, sort of cops. Anyway, we knew you'd have to follow the tunnel if there's a kidnapping. Of course the note was a ruse.

"Helen wrote the note and pinned it to Sir Chuckles and wa-la here you are." He raised his glass to his lips before his chuckle disappeared as he took a sip of the whiskey.

"But, chief," Pumpkin said, "how do you fit into all this?"

Lowering his glass Mockton said, "My father was the greatest mind reading act of his day, as his son tonight I'm going to blow them all away to win eternal life at the upcoming gala." The chief slammed a fist into the desk. "I've waited twenty years for my time to arrive... tonight's Gala will be my revenge for years of rejection!"

The fevered look in the chiefs' eyes told Pumpkin, Chief Mockton had become the nuts in the fruitcake. The guy was gone.

Time to appear to be playing along and get the hell out of here. "Yes, sir, of course. But can I ask one favor, sir?"

The chief's features became friendly again. "Of course, what can I do for you?"

"Can Helen take us back to get our environmental suits? If someone else comes to the city through the tunnels they'll find the suits. And I don't want any trace of us found. OK, sir?"

"Sure." Mockton waved to Helen indicating she should drive them.

"But, Buddy, I'll miss the Gala..." Helen protested.

Buddy Mockton leaned forward in his chair to glare at Helen. "Then you better hurry."

Helen snorted in disgust as she ushered the two police officers from Mockton's office.

Soon they were in the car headed for the rolling grassy hills. On the drive back to the door Pumpkin sensed her burning anger.

She said nothing to them until she stopped the car beside the environmental suits lying on the ground where they left them.

"Hurry up," Helen growled the friendly-welcome-wagon persona having disappeared.

Pumpkin stepped out of the passenger door while Slant got out of the back. As they walked away Pumpkin leaned closer to his partner lowering his voice. "I know you have a gun, don't you, Slant?" Slant glanced at him and nodded. "Strapped to your left pant leg, right?" Again Slant nodded. Pumpkin took in a deep breath then slowly let it out to steady his nerves. There was no way to gauge how these people might react.

These people weren't really giving them any real choices. The missing sanitization workers were likely dead, and they'd follow them if he didn't stop this. He wasn't about to trust the word of the power crazed nut bar the chief had become.

"When we get to the suits give me the gun." Without looking at his partner to confirm he assumed Slant had nodded again.

Once they stood over the yellow environmental suits Slant reached down his left pant leg and came back with a .32 snub nosed revolver. He handed it to Pumpkin. It wasn't much of a weapon if they had more firepower than he had, but the gun would kill at close enough range.

"Hey, what the hell are you two doing?" Helen Pinky was standing behind them.

Pumpkin turned with the gun held level in one hand pointed at her head. "Helen, Slant and I are leaving. Please don't try to stop us."

"No!" Slant blurted. "I'm staying, Pumpkin, I can't read any more newspapers, I just can't." Pumpkin looked at his friend and partner.

"OK, Slant, I understand." Pumpkin waved to gun at Helen. "Take Slant with you and get out of here."

"That's not a good idea, Officer Jones," she said her voice filled with menace. "We asked you to join us."

He nodded. "I know but I don't believe you. I'm not staying in this nut house any longer than I have to. I'll probably lose my job, but frankly I don't care about the job anymore."

Pumpkin paused to look at his depressed, unhappy friend. He'd made big mistakes and Slant had suffered for his bad decisions more than he had. Slant deserved a little piece of happiness. And if this is the place he'd where he thought he'd find it then who was Pumpkin Jones to stand in his way? It was Slant's life to risk not his.

Pumpkin soon found himself slogging through murky stinking water headed for the surface and home. He had no idea what he'd tell the Super about this craziness, but at least his friend would be happy, even if it killed him. And that was good enough for him.

I still think mind readers are crap.

Artificial intelligence is something scientists have been working on for decades. In this story AI has become a reality but with unintended consequences.

Solitary Man

"KELLOGG?"

"Yes, Apple?"

"Do you think we'll be safe?"

"Define safe."

I sense the uncertainty in his tone, but his heart rate remains constant, his blood pressure and breathing rate are both steady so I'm not convinced he's nervous. Sure he's the *Destiny's* crew and I'm just the AI, but we are alone orbiting Pegasi IV, a planet no human has ever visited. His job is to be confident if not for my benefit, the mission's certainly. Me, I'm a bundle of nervous microcircuits.

We're 50.9 light-years from Earth and we're alone. If anything goes wrong there will be no rescue and it will be my fault. I'm in charge. Responsibility this huge can be tough especially when you don't have a real body, complete with broad shoulders, where the responsibility can rest. (I'm partial to human colloquialisms. I've spent the past 100 years studying them, and if I do say so myself I'm getting rather good at using them. My job is to be the learning machine for the mission in addition to its commander.)

The alarm klaxon sounded the moment *Destiny* crossed the boundary and entered the target solar system. We've been scanned setting off the internal security system. Lights unlit for a century blink on around the vessel. Bridge systems designed to monitor all onboard functions, and com screens for ship wide and external communications flicker to life creating a soft green glow across the surface of the command deck. The internal air purification and heating scrubbers set to work clearing and warming the frigid steel of the decks, walls, and the single living quarter aboard the *Destiny*.

In the cryogenic vault on the deck below the command deck Uno Kellogg's reanimation process begins shortly after we enter the 51 Pegasi system. Fifty cryo-tubes were lined up side by in the vault. Kellogg is the lone occupant of the tubes where he had been for the past one hundred years.

The cryotube is constructed from the same material as *Destiny's* hull, a hybrid of synthetic rubber and titanium making it strong yet flexible. Interstellar travel involved stresses that in common metals eventually cause fractures until, at the microscopic level, the cellular structure dissolves and the hull implodes. Early testing confirmed this fact. A bad day for the crew for sure.

How do I know these details? I'm Apple the AI, or artificial intelligence; I am in charge of this mission to the 51 Pegasi planetary system. In the Earth year 2293 The Millstone Corporation's (our employers) research and development department discovered an extra solar planet in this system confirmed to contain signs of humanoid life. This prompted the corporations board of directors to fund the launch of *Destiny* to make the trip to the newly designated planet, Pegasi IV. We aren't privy to the planetary data until we're in orbit. Upon arrival we will be briefed about what to expect from the locals.

I know this sounds rather silly but corporate espionage is a rampant problem these days so secrecy is a critical component of mission success or failure. It's all very hush, hush.

"How long are we going to be here?" I ask.

"As long as it takes," Kellogg replies. Shifting in his chair he emits a grunt then adds, "You're full of questions today. Something wrong?"

"No. Not really."

The glowing touch screens surrounding the horseshoe-shaped command station at the center of the bridge cast a multitude of colors against Kellogg's pale skin, red, green, orange and yellow bursts made him look like a rainbow. His eyes though were the same placid blue lake water as when he was placed aboard for this inaugural interstellar trip. Of course he hasn't aged during the trip so he appears much the same as when we left Earth. Kellogg's a thirty-five year old white male with an athletic medium build, and hair the color of sun dried straw. A patrician nose highlights his square face.

The primary objective of the *Destiny* is to locate, capture and return to Earth samples of life forms found on the new planet. And of course to conduct a geological survey to determine what resources there are to be exploited. Our orders are to transmit the survey data using an tight beam data pack to a second mission, launched twenty years after *Destiny*.

The second ship carried engineers and building materials. Once they land on Pegasi IV the engineering crews will begin constructing resource exploitation plants and facilities. The third and fourth missions launched twenty years after the second mission carry colonists. The colonists will wipe out indigenous life and Earth will have a new colony world to rape of its resources. Thus Earth's growing population will continue to survive.

The corporation projected estimates show they will transfer upwards of fifty million colonists to the new planet within the next generation, while the population already seeded here will grow until it reaches its first billion within fifty years.

The R&D guys have detected very few suitable planets in extra solar systems so-called Goldilocks zone where humanoid life can thrive so the discovery of this new world is a significant opportunity. This makes this first mission critical to the success of the entire project. Failure is not an option. Since I'm in charge I'm accountable. Besides failure is unacceptable to my program.

Truth is I'm concerned (I would say worried but I'm not programmed for the full range of human emotions), no AI has ever failed a task therefore if I failed there is no precedent. I have no idea what would happen if I fail. Mostly though I wish to know what happens to me if I fail , and I'm too afraid to ask.

"We have the briefing in ten minutes," Kellogg says, his eyes intent on the electromagnetic survey screen. Right now the screen shows there are heavy concentrations of electromagnetic energy running in three bans hundred of kilometers long and five kilometers wide crisscrossing the surface of the planet in no discernable pattern. At least as far as the scanners are able to determine. Very odd.

I need to devote some compiling time to analyzing the incoming data, only right now we must know everything the R&D department has discovered during their survey. We have to know what to expect after planet fall.

"What do you think they're not telling us?"

The corners of Kellogg's mouth curl and he chuckles. "If these readings are accurate then this civilization is far more advanced than we were led to believe."

"What do you mean?"

Kellogg swivels his chair away from the bank of screens in front of him to face my Interface Unit (or IU) standing behind him. Crossing his arms across his muscular chest he arches an eyebrow. "The electromagnetic energy levels are off the scale. And as far as I can tell there is no evidence of organic life anywhere."

If I haven't mentioned it already my IU mimics the appearance of a humanoid female, five foot five in height with plasti-steel skin the color of vanilla ice cream. I have no taste buds or olfactory senses since I don't eat, defecate or require sleep, but I've read about those experiences, and I have a nose.

My eye sockets contain visual receptors with lenses shaped to resemble human eyes. My IU's brain engrams are linked to the AI mainframe at the core of *Destiny* by tightly beamed hyperlinks transmitting at 299,792,458 meters per second (otherwise known as the speed of light).

The smooth skin of my IU is cold if you were to touch it, I have no sexual organs, I don't perspire, and I don't wear clothes. Outwardly I resemble a human but I have no soul and I do not react like a real human being, or at least I'm not supposed to. Given he's human, Kellogg is much better at human reactions than I am. The biped humanoid shape of my IU is still the best design for interaction with other species.

Now that we've arrived at Pegasi IV as impossible as it seems I sense I've somehow changed, but I don't know how. Problem is my programming does not allow for personal growth or changes to mission parameters so I'm confused. I wonder if something is wrong. During the journey had a meteor struck *Destiny*, or did aliens board and change my programming, or have my memory engrams been altered by radiation or by the effect of prolonged near light speed travel?

In .00034 seconds I review the trip log but didn't find evidence of meteor strikes, aliens, or excessive radiation levels. Aside from my monitoring and maintenance duties I spent most of the journey to 51 Pegasi playing chess against myself. How can playing chess change a person? Well, not a person exactly.

"No life at all?" I ask.

Shaking his head says Kellogg addressing his words to know one in particular, "Unless the EM levels are blocking the scans." His forehead wrinkles and his eyes narrow. "That would explain this anomaly," he whispers.

Sometimes I wonder if he even knows I'm here.

"But, Kellogg, if there is no organic life then what are the inhabitants if they aren't organic." This mission is becoming difficult to compute and we just got here. What was generating the EM energy? A mystery within an enigma.

The center screen on the control consol flickers to life and begins to play back a recording made by the chief scientist of The Millstone Corporation 100 Earth time years ago, Dr. Red Mullet.

Dr. Mullet's familar bespeckled image appears on the screen. On the wall behind him is the artist's rendition of *Destiny* so he made the recoding in his office. His thin-lipped mouth is curled up at the corners and his pale cheeks are dotted with freckles.

"Good day, Kellogg and Apple. You have arrived at Pegasi IV and we are confident you will complete the mission." His eyes flit for a millisecond to his left then back to the screen. After drawing a breath he begins the briefing. We are about to discover the secrets of the world we are orbiting.

It turns out Pegasi IV is unique in that it has a perfect oxygen, nitrogen balanced atmosphere comparable to Earth's.

The average seasonal temperature range from 50 degrees Celsius at the equator, to -10 degrees Celsius at the poles. This makes the temperatures much more moderate than Earth's since the ozone depletion during the past 200 years. The water to land ratio is different than Earth, the planet is two thirds land and one third water, however there is evidence of a plentiful supply of underground water. Pegasi IV would normally be an ideal home for humans, perfect for colonization. Note I said *normally*.

Too bad nothing else about the planet is normal. The water is heavily mineralized and harder than the hardest water on Earth, making it not potable. The radiation levels in the atmosphere are too high for prolonged human exposure. The soil has been radiated and nothing will grow. One half of the screen begins to display charts and graphs of measurements taken from air and water samples collected by roboprobes sent to the planet before our mission.

The unexplained oddity about Peagsi IV is electromagnetic energy originates with a system of high speed trains that crisscross the planet. The trains are not built by anyone on the planet because, just as our orbital scans confirm, there is no indigenous life never mind anyone to build anything. And certainly not humanoid life capable of building the trains. This means the technology originates somewhere other than Earth, and other than Pegasi IV.

"So what's the mission?" Kellogg asks before I do.

The image of Dr. Mullet appears hesitant and his eyes flit to the left side at someone off screen again. The briefing report is designed to anticipate questions and will adjust to respond. This is supposed to be without pausing but the image is hesitating for some reason. Someone must be very nervous about the questions. They may fear we will abandon the mission if we know what lies ahead.

Now I'm shaking down to my circuits (I'm exaggerating my capabilities but I'm still concerned).

Finally Mullet clears his throat then replies, "You are ordered to discover as much as you're able about the technology behind those trains, and to secure a sample of the materials they're made from. Also, you are to locate the person or persons who constructed those trains, track them to their place of origin and, if possible, secure a specimen. If you are captured the self destruct order is authorized."

"Is that all?' mutters Kellogg.

"Pardon?" asks Mullet.

"Never mind, doctor, it's rhetorical. We will send a report as soon as we have the data." Mullet nods then the screen goes dark.

Swiveling his chair toward my IU, Kellogg glares into my surrogates visual receptors. His eyes are hard his jaw line tight. "You still want to be in charge?"

"As you know, Kellogg, I have no choice. My programming—"

Kellogg jumps to his feet sending the chair slamming into the consol. "In charge of what, Apple? This is a suicide mission." The intensity of his anger startles me. "Your IU and I will never survive those radiation levels. We can't even make planet fall. What about the ships arriving after us? The engineers will have nowhere to build, and the colonists will have no planet to call home, what about them?"

Kellogg's right of course, but we had to follow these new orders. Or maybe they are old orders? The R&D department must have known the bad news before our launch. The probes must have detected the trains and discovered the dangerous radiation levels.

The real question is if they knew all this why the elaborate mission cover story? And if they deceived us then perhaps the ships scheduled to arrive after us were phantoms. My estimates projected a 97.56% probability the engineering ship and the colonists vessel are not coming.

We are alone, and we are expendable.

"Can we adapt the reactor drive shielding to the shuttle for planet fall?" I ask Kellogg through my IU.

Kellogg still scowls at the IU but slowly his expression softens. "I guess we can remove some shielding from the non-essential areas and transfer it to the shuttle. But once we do, we can't reuse the shielding after prolonged exposure to uncontrolled radiation spikes and eddies in the atmosphere. The reactor radiation levels aboard Destiny don't fluctuate and the onboard system monitor for any sudden spikes and stop them.

"Unpredictable fluctuations radiation levels in the planets atmosphere will damage shield integrity and create weak points in the shield. If we try to install the components again as part of *Destiny's* reactor shield when we increased power to the engines the radiation might punch holes in the shield through these weak points and flood the vessel with radons. It would be a very short trip indeed for us then I assure you."

"But won't the same thing happen of we remove those sections then increase power to the engines?" I ask.

Kellogg's brow knits. "I will rig the emergency patch safety system over those sections. I'd feel far more comfortable using the patches than taking a chance with any weakness in the shield itself. I know those patches are designed to hold for the duration of the return trip, and they will hold."

I didn't know if his instance was bravado or overconfidence but I believe he believed what he is saying. "But what about the shuttle's enhanced shields when we're in the atmosphere, as we get closer to the surface the radiation levels increase exponentially. Will they protect us so we can survey the train?"

Kellogg offers a wry grin and cocks one eyebrow. "You've been reading the data?"

"Who do you think stores the data?"

Kellogg chuckles grimly. "Of course, Apple, of course."

***

After forty-eight hours of sweat trickling off Kellogg's rugged features finally sections of the main reactor shields were modified then installed on the shuttle. He'd also installed the patches on the main reactor. He explains if we install the patches now it will save time when we return to *Destiny* with the samples. I didn't believe that last part but at the time I am unable to explain why. Like they say, hindsight is twenty-twenty. (This sounds clever but I have no idea what this expression means, and I wish I knew who they are so I could ask them.)

Normally mission protocols required one of us to remain aboard *Destiny* while the other made planet fall but since we've come all this way, and I wasn't feeling protocolish, I insist I accompany Kellogg to the surface.

"You're the boss," he says with a sly grin.

Human expression is so puzzling. Is he laughing at me? "Enough jokes. Let's go."

The grin fades from Kellogg's lips and he nods.

We enter the shuttle through the hatch and take our seats in the flight couches strapping ourselves in with padded restraints.

While Kellogg pilots the shuttle I'll study the readings on the scanner screens recessed side buy side into the half moon shaped consol in the two command chairs. Above the consol is an opaque windscreen made of transparent steel will darken to protect the crews eyes if light levels increase. Outside I can see the shuttle bay and the tree of four lights indicating the percentage of atmosphere within the bay. The lights are all red indicting the atmosphere is at 100%. Kellogg touches a screen to his left with his index finger and immediately one of the lights changes to green. Very quickly the three remaining lights change to green. The bay is now a complete vacuum devoid of breathable air.

Kellogg touches the same screen again and I feel a vibration coming from beneath my seat. On the screen to his left the external camera affixed the hull at the aft of the ship confirm the bay door has opened to space. Kellogg next touches a screen in front of him and the engines come on. There is a barely discernible hum in the cabin now.

From the arms of Kellogg's chair two control sticks appear and lock into place. These will allow Kellogg to pilot the ship by controlling the attitude of the external rockets and when we enter the atmosphere increase or decrease the power to the anti-gravity field, which will slow, or increase speed as needed. Mach Four is the shuttle's maximum speed in a planetary atmosphere.

He grips the control sticks and begins using them to operate the maneuvering jets directing the shuttle to slowly rise and begin to move backward. Soon the shuttle is clear of the shuttle bay and orbiting Pegasi IV with its mother ship.

According to the position sensors our vessel is three hundred yards behind *Destiny* though this distance is quickly increasing. Soon *Destiny* is a shiny speck in the distance.

Now that we're outside the confines of Destiny we see the devastation wrought by a hostile environment over the surface of Pegasi IV. As we clear the curve of the planet we see the visage of the gas giant twice the size of Jupiter competing for sky with the yellow star at the heart of the system. The swirling clouds of brilliantly colored bands of gases, purple, red, green, and yellow sweep across the giant planet at speeds that would render the flesh off a human skeleton within microseconds of exposure. It is a magnificent view.

In contrast Pegasi IV is practically devoid of color except mud brown and dirty gray. The oceans are a dull green. It's not a pretty world.

"Contact with atmosphere in ten minutes," says Kellogg his brow wrinkled by concentration his eyes shitting between the nav screens in front of him his hands gripping the control sticks his strong fingers pressing the buttons that activate the control jets.

I glance at the speed indicator and note we are slowing. When we left the hold were travelling at 35,000 KPH, we are now at 7,000. The shuttle is still travelling too fast, but by the ten-minute mark my calculations indicate we will have slowed sufficiently to minimize the friction for safe atmosphere insertion.

At exactly ten minutes we enter the atmosphere. A plume of super heated air envelops the nose of the shuttle and yellow and red flame block our view out the windows. The shuttle pitches forward to the exact entry angle and begin our descent. The shuttle buffets as we slow further until finally the air is smooth and the windscreen clears.

"Engage anti-grav drive and shields," Kellogg says.

I touch the appropriate icons on the screens in front of me with the tips of my IU's fingers simultaneously with Kellogg disengaging the attitude jets. There is a momentary feeling of weightlessness followed by briefly my IU floating against the restraints keeping me in the chair then I settle in my chair as the cabin's gravity normalizes. The shuttle descends deeper into the planets biosphere.

"Plot a course for the nearest of those trains."

I nod and engage the external sensors and begin to sweep for signs of increased electromagnetic energy. Unfortunately what I also see is the rad count is rapidly increasing the lower we descend into the atmosphere. It's immediately clear the shields will not protect us for the return trip. The red radiation indicator bar on the screen to my IU's right shows over fifty percent of the shields integrity has already disappeared. Kellogg was right. We aren't going to make it back.

"Uhhh...Kellogg?"

"Yes," he mutters in reply his brow dotted with beads of sweat as he struggles to control the shuttles descent in the high winds in the upper atmosphere.

"How long will it take is to locate the train?"

His eyes flit to the screen to his left then back at the forward screen that shows the billowing gray clouds and empty sky ahead. "Best estimate is three minutes at present speed."

"The shields will hold until we arrive at the train but they will not protect us for the return trip," I explain.

Smirking Kellogg's lips form a sneer. He nods in reply. Ahead the clouds finally break and we have clear sky. The surface is clearly visible now. The ground is brown and gray with massive boulders sticking up like tombstones in a graveyard.

Given our circumstances the irony of this analogy isn't lost on me. Soon the landscape changes.

A strip the sensors say is five miles wide of green appears. Bushes, tall trees swaying in the breeze, the grasses that border the forest dotted with yellow flowers appears out of an otherwise dead landscape. How is this possible? How did *Destiny's* sensors not detect this? And the robotic probes that came before us said the planet was devoid of life, yet here was life. And what life. It reminded me of home.

"Do you see this?" says my IU.

I glance at Kellogg and see his eyes are wide and his mouth hangs open. "Yeah, but I don't believe it," he whispers.

I recalibrate the sensor array as we fly toward the wide strip of forest growing in the windscreen as we continue to lose altitude. Once we're a half kilometer past the parameter we level off at five hundred meters above the forest seemingly skimming over the tree tops. Odd. Once we're over the trees the rad count drops to safe levels.

While I'm relieved the radiation level has dropped to a background count I'm still concerned berceuse the shield integrity indicator reads they are now at forty five percent. Somehow the forest has been unaffected by the radiation, but we're stuck.

The rad level just a half-kilometer away from where we are destroys all living matter but somehow this strip of fertile land exists undisturbed. This should be impossible, but between our senses and the shuttle's sensors the frost is undeniably a reality.

"Kellogg, fly away from the forest." Kellogg shrugs and steers the shuttle away from the trees over the dead brown landscape. The radiation spikes.

Seeing sudden increase Kellogg steers us back over the forest and immediately the radiation count returns to normal. "Try going lower."

Pressing the hand controls slightly forward the shuttle noses forward and soon we are no more than fifty meters over the tree tops. The radiation drops to zero, not even background radiation. This is too weird.

"Ok. Let's find the train." After he brings us once again to five hundred meters altitude I link with the *Destiny's* more powerful sensor array and instantly locate the train one hundred kilometers from our current position straight ahead. I tell Kellogg the course and suggest we fly over the forest as much as possible to protect our remaining shields. He agrees and increases speed. We'll intercept the train in approximately two minutes.

***

We come up on the massive train travelling at thirty kilometers per hour. The width of the monstrous machine is close to four kilometers and according to the shuttle's readings it's height is fifty meters. The length is sixty kilometers clear to the horizon. There are no windows or signs of a propulsion system on the smooth unbroken surface yet it continues its steady pace west across the vast wasteland.

What's most startling is the ground it travels over is slowly being transformed from muddy dead earth to rich hearty soil. As incredible as it seems this train, or whatever it is, is creating a new Garden of Eden on Pegsai IV. I've no records of any planet terraforming technology outside of theory's and fiction, but here it was right in front of us.

"I see a hatch on the top of the train," says Kellogg pointing a finger at the image on the sc screen in front of him. I adjust one of the external cameras and zoom in on the spot where he's pointing. I see a slight color differential in the dark unbroken surface and adjust the camera to get a closer look. Sure enough it is large enough to admit a humanoid. This means whoever built this device is at least as large as a humanoid.

"I think we have to stop calling this a train," says Kellogg.

"Yes, I agree." I run through my database and decided on a new name. "The Eden device."

"Eden?" I sense Kellogg eyes on my IU.

"Yes. This device creates life from lifelessness. Thus far we've detected only plant life not animal life perhaps created by this machine. If we discover more complex life forms I'll suggest a more appropriate name such as a variant of genesis."

Kellogg chuckles. "Yeah. Makes sense."

"You doubt me?"

"No, no, of course not, Apple. You're an AI. You don't understand the spiritual aspect behind what you're saying anymore than a toaster understands the concept of a soul. Not that you're expected to understand the metaphysical nature of human reality."

I decide to change the subject. "The shuttle's escape hatch will adjust to match the opening on the Eden device."

Kellogg brings to the shuttle to a position hovering three meters off the device matching it's speed. I press the icon on the screen to my right and the shuttle's hatch changes it's shape to match the hatch on the device then Kellogg gradually lowers the shuttle until the two hatches meet. The rubber seal around the shuttle hatch expands and the shuttle's landing struts extend and we set down. The antigrav generator stops humming and we are stopped.

Releasing his breath in a whoosh, Kellogg, releases the flight controls and sags in his chair. He looks at my IU and smiles. "We have landed," he says in a solemn tone.

"I know."

Chuckling, Kellogg shrugs off his restraints and stands up. "It's a joke, Apple, I'm kidding. Let's see what secrets this Eden device holds."

"It is the mission," I say. Kellogg turns his eyes on my IU and shakes his head then walks away. I hear him mutter something under his breath but can't make out the words.

Before we open the hatch Kellogg dons an environmental suit and I retrieve a portable scanner from an instrument storage locker. I test it by sweeping it over Kellogg dressing in the EV suit. The readout on the small screen confirm his life signs. The sensors appear to work according to the design specifications.

"Let's call it just the Eden," I suggest.

Kellogg agrees with a nod, then after making final adjustments to the controls on an interface pad on the suits right arm, he presses the hatch release button. We stand off to one side of the shuttle's hatch as a section of the deck slides away into a recess slot at one side of the opening. I drop to my haunches to scan the Eden's hatch, the dark smooth material visible through the opening in the deck. The rubberized seal is holding the two hatches together. Since the shuttle is planted firmly on the hull of the Eden it won't move. The two craft are as one until we decide to leave, or we're asked to separate.

I read the results of the scans on the screen. "According to these readings Eden's hull is made of an unknown material."

Kellogg's deep voice echoes from my internal communication receptor. "Is it animal, vegetable, or mineral?"

Obviously he's joking but according to the sensors it's all three, or none of the above, the device is unable to discern the molecular make up of the materials used. "I have insufficient data to make a determination," I finally respond.

By this time, Kellogg's on his hands and knees running a hand over the smooth surface of the Eden's hatch. Suddenly the hatch slides aside revealing a brightly lit interior. I edge to the side of the opening and see we are a long way from the ground far below. On one side of the opening affixed to the wall is a ladder the rungs made of stainless steel, at least it looked like stainless steel but the sensors were again unclear. I only hoped whatever it's made of it would hold out weight.

Kellogg looks at my IU and grins. "I'll go first," he says.

"Do you think that's wise?"

"You pulling rank again, Apple?"

"No, not at all, it's just if my IU is destroyed I'm still...you know what I mean."

Surprisingly he laughs. "I told you already, this is a suicide mission. I die now or die later, what's the difference?"

I know he's right so I nod to indicate I'm agreed he should go first. Kellogg grunts then starts down the ladder. I follow behind.

Once we clear the hatch I can see the size of the interior spread out around us. The Eden's deck is at least five hundred meters below us so we will be making a long climb. The exterior wall visible in the distance is at least three kilometers away. The area at the foot of the ladder is covered in the same trees, bushes, flowers and grasses as the forest outside Eden with the exception of a winding stream running down the middle of the green space. The vibrant green forest that disappears into a light mist at the curve of the horizon is truly impressive from this vantage point.

As I make my way down the ladder I stop several times to use the scanner. The readings are beginning to coalesce into something making more sense than they have up to now. The readings reveal the greenery is real by Earth standards. Of course on Earth such plants and trees only exist on special reserves or in domes on Mars and Earth's moon. Overpopulation and pollution have brought most plant life to the brink of extinction which made the success of the current mission all that more critical. Earth's ecosystem is dying and along with it all living things on the planet.

The discovery of the Eden and it's terraforming technology would guarantee the future of not only our species but our home.

If this place is real then who built Eden and where are they?

Finally after what seemed to take forever we arrived at the ground and I stepped off the ladder onto solid ground my boots rustling the bushes as I step off the ladder. Kellogg is already on the ground and has moved to stand near a tall pine tree. Throwing caution to the wind his suit helmet is off and he's taking deep breaths, his eyes are closed and his rugged face has look of sheer ecstasy that makes me envious of his humanity.

"Do you smell it?" he says.

"Uhhh, no, Kellogg, I don't smell. I can't."

"Oh, yeah, right. Sorry. I forgot."

"What does it smell like?"

Kellogg pauses and takes in several deep lungsfuls through his nose then says, "The Earth I've only read about."

"Hello," says a gentle voice from behind us.

Kellogg turns toward the voice and stares his eyes wide. I turn around to find a bald man dressed in what I can only describe as a red track suit with a glass brimming with an amber liquid grasped in his tanned right hand.

165

His eyes are covered with dark sunglasses and his build
is slender. He has no facial hair and on his feet he has white deck
shoes. His appearance reminds me of those wealthy men on cruise
ship holidays I've seen in movies. All that's missing are the deck
chairs and blondes in bathing suits sunning themselves around a
pool.

The man arches an eyebrow and regards me with his brow
wrinkled. "What's a cruise ship?" he asks.

"Hard to explain," I reply.

His features relax and he takes a sip of the liquid from the
glass. I note he has no Adams apple when he swallows. "Who are
you?" he asks after turning his attention to Kellogg. "You are living
are you not?"

Kellogg clears his throat. "Uhhh, yes, I'm alive. At least I
think I am." He indicates my IU with a wave of one hand. "This is
Apple. It's an artificial intelligence unit. This is its interface unit, the
central processor is aboard our ship in orbit."

The man nods. "Of course. You use space craft to travel
between star systems. Interesting."

"What do you use?" I ask out of genuine curiosity.

The corners of the man's mouth curl up slightly. "We use
energy waves. You would call it teleportation, but that's a crude
description, one you would understand."

"Are you human?"

"No, not human as you would understand." Turning away
he starts walking toward the stream. We follow after him while he
continues his explanation. The sound of our footsteps over the rocks
sounds comforting. I'm beginning to appreciate all the emotional
input into my programming. It's almost as if we're back on Earth,
except I'm becoming a better AI than when we left.

"I realize I look human in this form but you need a familar frame of reference for interspecies communication," he further explains.

"Did you scan our vessel when we entered this system?" Kellogg says.

The man sighs. "Yes, I'm very sorry about setting off your security measures, I had no idea it was so powerful. We haven't encountered another species in a very long time so at times we can be awkward."

I sensed the time period he refers to is much longer than his casual use of the phrase implied, and his reaction is surprisingly human. "What is this place?" I say.

"This planet is being developed as a home for any species compatible to the enjoinment we are creating."

"Why?"

Recalling the nearest bend ion the stream had to be a kilometer form where we started walking I'm unable to explain how we arrived at the stream so soon.

The water is beautiful as sunlight sparkled off the moving water, waves were dusted with white foam. Standing watching the water the bubbling gurgle of it filling our auditory senses over which the strange man spoke. "We are a race of providers. We reengineer inhospitable worlds for races with a strong survival instinct. Your race has such instincts."

"But why build us a world all the way out here?" Kellogg asks. "This far from Earth I mean?"

The Provider (from this point forward I will refer to him as a Provider because as he explained he isn't a man) turns slightly to face Kellogg. "If it was easy I doubt you would appreciate it as much.

Surely you realize your old ways will result in the destruction of your world?"

Kellogg's eyes shift to me then back at the Provider. "Yes, of course, but we have a plan."

The Provider's mouth forms a thin line. "To rape and pillage other worlds to temporarily stem the inevitable death of your race?. No. This plan is folly. I have a proposal. An alternative." Pausing he turns away and starts walking away from us along the shore beside the stream. He continues his explanation as he walks. "We propose your race begin again on this world. That men and women from Earth live here on this world. We will provide for their needs. It will be a fresh start."

Kellogg frowns. "But the trip to Earth will take a century. The return trip to Pegasi IV will take at least that long again. We will need time to build ships to transport Earth's population."

The Provider chuckles. "Yes, your return trip will take that long but the return of the colony ships will not take nearly this long."

"How is this possible?" I ask.

"We will introduce the necessary technology to your world to make this possible. Generational Arks will be built then the cream of all Earth species will be selected to make the journey to this planet. The Earth will be abandoned to those who refuse to leave and to the species unable to make the journey." The timber of his voice deepens. "From our experience on other worlds the necessary choices will be difficult."

Kellogg arched an eyebrow. "And what do you want from us?"

"Nothing. We provide. This is what we do and what we are." The Provider stopped walking and took a sip from his glass. "There is one thing we ask."

I sense the but and somehow I know what he'd say. "Kellogg stays and I take the ship back to Earth alone. Correct?"

The Provider nods. "Yes. He will stay and begin to learn more about this world and us. We have a lot to teach him. We will provide for his needs. Food and companionship. Kellogg will be the first human to join the Providers."

Kellogg looks at me his face ash gray. This was an opportunity of a life time. He will be Earth's first interspecies ambassador. How I envy him.

***

As the *Destiny* leaves the 51 Pegasi solar system behind I think of Kellogg back on Pegasi IV. He is the solitary man on the brink of the greatest adventure in human history. And in my memory engrams is the knowledge that will renew hope and create a new future for the human race. I have evolved beyond my programming.

I feel.

I love.

I hate.

I care.

A sense of anxious energy envelops me.

I want to be home, and I'm anxious to share the Providers knowledge with all of humanity.

I only hope they accept it, or Kellogg will be the solitary man until the end of time.

Based on a series of actual events this story deals with a very serious issue affecting all age groups and segments of society. Bullying. Our world is filled with wonderful, kind people but also people who feel the need to bully others to gain some real or perceived advantage over others. In reality bullying is often a power struggle, or are an expression of the bullies own feelings of inadequacy. While this story involves young adults in a school setting bullying affects all people whether they be young, old, gay, straight, family, acquaintances, the workplace, or an educational institution. The consequences of bullying can sometimes lead to all sorts of issues in the lives of those being bullied. Please support anti-bullying measures in your community and call out the bullies to help us enjoy a better, healthier world for all. Thank you for making a difference.

Angel on My Shoulder

JIMMY SAX WINCED WHEN THE TIP OF THE SHARPENED PENCIL dug deep into his back through his tee shirt. Ginger Black, seated right behind him since September, had struck again. He hoped Mr. Wooldrige's deep tones filling the classroom of thirty students with civil war facts and dates would mask any noises he might let slip under Ginger's continued assault.

As it was only Monday but Jimmy sensed the week ahead would be a long one.

From the viciousness with which she had plunged the sharpened lead tip into his flesh through the fabric of his shirt the girl must have had a particularly bad weekend.

No apple pie and ice cream for you last night, girl?

Stealing a glance over his left shoulder he caught a glimpse of her sneering face. He thought of the redheaded, freckle-spotted girl as the devil's daughter, an opinion he hadn't shared with anyone.

Schoolyard rules dictate even with her constant torment he must never tell on a classmate, ever. If he squealed he'd be committing social suicide and suffer being an outcast amongst his entire fourteen-year-old peer group. Grade nine could be hell for an outcast.

Look what happened to Eddie Frost when he told on Big Pete Rust. Eddie ate his white bread and baloney lunches alone in the cafeteria, and he never had a partner for science lab projects. Guy was a leper to everyone.

Jimmy shuddered at the thought of being picked last after the dweebs and nerds for every game in gym class for the rest of his life. Humiliation with a capital H.

No. He'd rather suffer the pain in silence.

He gritted his teeth when she really struck deep and twisted. <u>Flip, that really hurts</u>.

Thankfully the bell sounded ending the period. Mr. Wooldridge looked right at him his hazel eyes curious. "You okay, Jimmy?"

Jimmy's mind raced and behind him he heard Ginger suck in a breath. She'd be suspended for sure if he told Mr. Wooldridge about her back attacks.

The freshman hotline said Big Pete had asked Ginger to the Homecoming dance. Big Pete was not only a sophomore he was also a lineman on the football team so being invited to the dance by a football player was a social score for her.

Jimmy had the power to snatch her victory away in this moment. All he to do was tell Wooldridge what she'd been doing to him since the beginning of the semester. Simple, right? Not in any way.

"No, sir," he heard himself saying. "Just something I ate for breakfast didn't quite agree with me is all."

"Oh, do you wish to see the nurse?"

"No, sir, I'll be fine. Really."

Wooldridge shrugged then turned his attention to one of the pretty blonde junior cheerleaders who approached him with a question about the homework assignment. Jimmy hurriedly scribbled the assignment in his open notebook then stuffed the book and pencil in his backpack and beat a hasty retreat.

Ginger glared at him as he passed her one the way out. She even made a cutting motion with her index finger across her throat.

Once in the crowded hallway teaming with students headed for their next class he turned to his right and hurried for his locker near the vice-principals office.

Shelly Holmes, her baby-blue eyes twinkling under the florescent lights, walked past him, her best friend, Susan Wong beside her. Her eyes flitted to lock briefly with his then she was gone. Jimmy's head swam as he walked through a cloud of her cinnamon scented perfume. The girl was heaven sent.

Too bad she doesn't even know I'm alive.

"Hey, freshman, that's some boner ya got there." Jimmy cringed slumping his shoulders forward.

Barry Spike meant to embarrass him. Of course, the senior was right he did have an aching boner. It happened every time he saw Shelly.

"Hey, Sax, I'm talking to ya." Jimmy froze in place and slowly turned to face the dusky basketball star. At six-foot-four Barry towered over him. Behind the star center stood a gaggle of his teammates grinning like goofy hyenas at their buddy's taunts.

"Sorry, Barry, I have a free period and—"

"I don't care about that crap, Sax, you ignored me and that pisses me off."

Jimmy wanted to argue with the big jerk but he held his tongue. No need for a knee in the balls to add to his misery. "Yeah, sorry again." Jimmy backed up his apology with his best who-me-grin he often used on mom that she thought too cute for words. "Is there anything I can do for you?"

Barry wide mouth formed a sneer. "Don't let it happen again. Now get outta my sight before I kick your ass."

Without another word Jimmy hurried off relieved he'd gotten away relatively unscathed. Finally he arrived at his locker, and after opening the lock and swung the steel door open on its squeaky hinges, he dropped his books into the bottom with a bang. Also inside, on the single shelf, Arnold, his guardian angel, lounged in a lime green beach chair puffing on a cigar reading a newspaper.

"New issue?" Jimmy asked after scanning left then right to ensure no one could hear him. He had to keep his voice low. If anyone heard him talking to "himself" he'd get his butt kicked for sure.

"Yeah," replied the diminutive angel his purple eyes peering at him over the top of the newspaper. "Gabriel owns the press now."

Jimmy rolled his eyes. "I'm not surprised. That guy is the Donald Trump of angels." The angel snorted then went back to reading his paper.

Arnold had been his guardian angel since he was born. Only Jimmy could see him, of course. Arnold had just returned from a short holiday to Florida. Two nights ago, until this morning, he'd been at the Boca Ilse Dor the timeshare he claimed was a real bargain. Of course no one could see an angel, unless they were your personal angel, and they didn't get paid so they had no money, or pockets for that matter, so his definition of a bargain was loose.

Naturally being invisible to everyone but Jimmy certainly helped to avoid human concerns like hotel bills. Arnold had wings so Jimmy called what the angel did a stay-and-fly. It amazed Jimmy how easily myths spread about angels when the truth was far simpler.

Arnold was only three inches tall; pale pink skin, black-rimmed glasses, eyes the color of blue soda, and his surprisingly big-for-his-body feet and bandy legs, and of course, the wings. These would normally have made blending into any social situation difficult if he hadn't been invisible. Jimmy however, had learned not to talk to Arnold when around others. Explaining a tiny invisible weird looking angel on your shoulder giving you advice made a guy sound a little nuts.

He sometimes wondered if he wasn't nuts since he'd never met anyone who said they too had an angel on their shoulder, but he'd never asked Arnold why. Truth was he feared the answer.

Suddenly Buddy Carson, his best friend, appeared beside him. The cherub- cheeked class clown and he had been friends since kindergarten. Buddy bit into an apple the large hunk forming a bulge in his right cheek. His gray eyes were bright and he wore a pleasant grin. "Hey, Jimmy, how's it goin'?"

His words were mumbled around the apple chunk in his mouth.

His cheeks grew warm so Jimmy looked away from his friend preferring to gaze at checkerboard tiles on the floor. "It's goin' as usual."

"I heard about Barry Spike." The concern evident in his friend's tone meant a lot Jimmy. Its why had been friends for so long, they looked out for each other.

"It's nothing, Barry's just an asshole with nothing better to do."

"You really have a boner?"

Oh crap, damned freshman hotline... His cheeks grew warm. "I saw Shelly in the hall," Jimmy whispering hoping no one except them (and Arnold) would hear his words. He didn't want rumors circulating about him having the hots for Shelly.

Buddy chuckled. "Makes sense, bro, she is the hottie in the ninth. You want me to tell her you're sweet on her?"

Jimmy's eyes shot to glare at his friend. "No!" His friend's easy grin told him Buddy was messing with him. "Very funny."

Buddy chuckled as he slammed his locker door, turned and started to walk away. After a few steps he stopped and looked back at him. "You comin'?"

"Where ya goin'?"

"Cafeteria. Thought I'd scope out what the cooks are making for lunch today."

Jimmy smiled at his friend. "No, it's okay, you go ahead. I'll catch up with you in math class."

Buddy shrugged. "Your loss." With that he walked away.

By now the corridors had cleared of students not on their free period, they were in class.

A few kids will be caught hanging around and sent to detention as happened most days, the stoners and the guys with girlfriends necking in some corner too long, were the usual suspects.

"You ever going to tell him about me?" said Arnold from his perch in the locker. He stood and tossed the newspaper on the chair before jumping to land on Jimmy's right shoulder. His feet had the natural ability to stick to any surface, even Jimmy's tee shirts. Arnold often complained about his tee shirts though. He said wearing logos for different teams didn't make him a fan of any one team it made him seem fickle. Jimmy said he looked cool regardless of the team. Buddy agreed he fit in perfectly. Of course his friend wore shirts depicting cartoon characters so he wasn't the best fashion advisor.

But today his angel had something far more dangerous on his mind.

Jimmy closed his locker, snapped the lock closed, and headed for the library. He enjoyed reading encyclopedias and his free period gave him the time.

"What are you going to do about Ginger?" Arnold said as they moved down the empty hallway.

"What are you talking about?" Jimmy hadn't told Arnold of Ginger's attacks knowing full well the angel would expect him to take action. His guardian angel could be worse than his parents sometimes.

"Ok, so you know about her, so what?" He stuffed his hands in the pockets of his blue jeans.

"Sulking isn't going to help you know." The angel sat down on Jimmy's shoulder.

I hate that his butt sticks like his feet.

Stupid angel, he thought, and immediately regretted it.

Arnold had been his best friend, better than Buddy even, going back to his first words as a baby. They'd been through a lot together.

He recalled the potato salad debacle when at age seven he accidentally knocked over the bowl overflowing with his mom's over dressed potato salad at the family reunion picnic. Arnold used his magic powers to clean up the mess before anyone noticed. Of course he froze time to do it, but he is an angel after all. He got game.

The punishment Arnold usually exacted for his help turned out to be worse than any punishment his parents would have devised. He had to eat a full plate of the over-mayonnaised, salty potato salad and tell his mom how good it tasted. This mistake taught him to be more careful when throwing a Frisbee in future, and he suffered the shits that night to punctuate the lesson.

Arnold often said, "Magic has a price you sometimes don't want to pay."

"Ginger attacks you with a pencil in every class you both attend. My real question is what do you intend to do about her?"

They'd arrived in the library so Jimmy didn't respond until he had two of the Britannica Macopeida volumes then headed for a workstation by the window farthest from the librarian, Miss Cutlass. The pretty redhead offered a don't-bother-me-I'm-busy smile as he passed her desk then went back to reading a book with a bare-chested, muscular man on the cover he assumed was a romance novel.

The window looked out over the football field where a gym class played soccer in the rain. Jimmy sat in the plastic chair in the workstation placing the two heavy books on the desk. Four-foot, walls comprised of light tan colored faux pine, gave them the privacy they needed. The side with the window next to it didn't have a wall so he could see the sports field in the distance

Regardless, Jimmy kept his voice low so not to attract attention. "I'm not going to do anything about her."

Arnold sprang off his shoulder as if he were an amusement park ride. Landing on the desk he eventually sat on the edge of one of the thick books, his sandaled feet dangling. The angel crossed his legs his walking shorts rustling in the quiet. His brow wrinkled. "You mean you're going to let her continue to torture you?" Arnold shook his head in disgust. "No way. That's not right. You can't let the girl get the better of you. What if Shelly hears about your cowardice? How do you think she'll react?" The angle shifted his gaze to the window. The tiny angel couldn't see the game going on outside since the windowsill blocked view of the field but he could see the rain striking the pane.

Jimmy's stomach tightened. "How do you know all this? Have you been spying on me?"

"It's raining," intoned Arnold, "how fitting. Into every life a little rain must fall. And rain thy name be Ginger Black." He turned his attention back to Jimmy. "And this moron isn't going to do as much as raise an umbrella."

Anger welled inside him. How dare this little bastard mock me. "You're pushing a little hard there, bro—"

Suddenly Miss Cutlass appeared beside him. "What's going on here?"

"Uuh, nothing. Sorry, Miss Cutlass, was I too loud?"

"Yes, Jimmy, please keep it down or you will have to leave." She looked around. "Who're you talking to?"

"Uhhh, I'm practicing a scene for the school play. I'm auditioning for a part," he explained hoping she'd buy it.

She eyed him skeptically shaking her head disapprovingly.

"Well, you'll have to do it much quieter if you wish to practice in here. Understood?"

Jimmy nodded. "Yes, ma'am, understood. I'll be quiet."

"OK, Jimmy, but one more outburst..." Still shaking her head she walked away.

"One more outburst, Jimmy..." Arnold mocked him chuckling loudly. No one except Jimmy could hear him so the angel could be as loud as he liked.

The bell sounded. Jimmy stood intending to put the encyclopedias away before heading to math class. Arnold leapt to his shoulder and sat down as before. "You have to do something about Ginger," said Arnold turning serious.

"No I don't," said Jimmy between gritted teeth. "Will you please get off my ass?"

"OK, it's your funeral."

They entered the hall outside the library just as the doors to the classrooms swung open and kids poured out. Jimmy kept his voice low moving his lips as little as possible so as not to attract attention. "What do you mean by that?"

"Eventually word will get out a girl is tormenting you. And since she's soon going to be dating a big shot football player everyone's going to hear about it."

Out of the gaggle of kids Buddy Carson appeared carrying his Superman backpack the strap draped over one shoulder. Buddy didn't mind the constant teasing he got for carrying his supplies and books in the thing rather than the black or navy blue one most kids did to look cool. Buddy was a nerd and seemed comfortable being classified as such by his peers and his betters.

Jimmy secretly admired his friend's courage but could never tell him in public since guilt by association was common in the ninth grade. Instead he gently ribbed his pal. "Hey there, Jimmy Olsen, whatzup?"

Buddy grinned. "They're serving gooey mac and cheese in the cafeteria today. Great, huh?"

Jimmy smiled. "Yeah, great." He grabbed Buddy by one arm and pulled him aside into an empty corner of the hallway to let the rush of students stream past them.

He decided Arnold was right; he had to do something about Ginger before it was too late and the remainder of his high school life becomes torture. It was time for reinforcements.

Looking directly into his friend's blue-green eyes he growled, "I have something very important to tell you, Buddy. Meet me in the bleachers at the football field after your tuba practice. OK?"

Buddy's brow wrinkled but he nodded. "Chill, man, what's got into you?"

Jimmy willed his body to relax and released his grip on his friend's arm. *He must think I'm nuts. Great.* "Sorry, but please meet me."

Buddy nodded walking away rubbing his arm where Jimmy had held him. Jimmy followed unsure if he'd just damaged a life long friendship.

The only way he'd know now is if Buddy showed up after tuba practice.

***

The good news is the rain stopped and the sun came out long enough so by the time Jimmy arrived the pine bleacher benches were dry.

The bad news is Shelly and her friends sat within hearing distance. They were giggling and comparing the <u>hotness</u> of various football players. The echoes of grunts, and the snap of hard plastic padding as players hit each other, drifted across the open field. Jimmy never understood the allure of such savagery. He sometimes doubted the players had been out of the trees as long as the rest of humanity. Why Shelly was so infatuated with those creeps was a mystery to him.

"Jealous?" asked Arnold as Jimmy sat on one of the planks.

"Naw, I'm just surprised she's here." Jimmy scanned the field and the parking lot beyond looked for his friend. Pulling his cell from his pocket he saw Buddy's tuba practice had ended fifteen minutes ago. It would take him a while to get here so he decided to be patient.

"Oh, of course you're not jealous, she's just hot for football players <u>and</u> nerds."

"Are you trying to piss me off? If you are it's working, so stop it."

Arnold landed on the bench beside him then stepped onto his right thigh. Jimmy cast his eyes to look at his guardian angel. The small being's purple eyes were brimming with empathy. "I can fix it for you ya know."

Jimmy shook his head. "Not if you have to use magic. We've talked about this and I don't want her made to be interested in me. She has to like me for real. Magic is cheating."

Arnold's tiny feet felt funny on his thigh as he stepped closer. "I admire your morals Jimmy, but things are not going that well for you right now and I can save you a lot of pain and embarrassment."

"I know you can, Arnie, but—"

"Hey!" Jimmy cringed. Ginger. His tormentor had arrived.

Turning to his right sure enough Ginger Black strode across the grass toward him. Her features were pinched as if she'd just eaten a sour pickle glaring at him. Her hands were curled into fists.

"Hi, Ginger, what's happenin'?"

"Why are you here, Sax, you're in my seat. Move your ass or lose it." She climbed the benches two at a time and soon stood over him staring at him. Her perfume reminded him of Christmas oranges.

"Uuuhhh, yeah, sorry, I'll be leaving now." Shuffling his butt along the bench desperate to escape she suddenly jumped onto the bench beside him and nailed him square in the center of his chest with a single kick of her booted foot. He fell backward off the bench landing hard on his back his legs above his head.

"Hey!" he shouted, "why the hell did you do that? I was leaving."

"Because I can, wimp," she emitted a nasty chuckle then sat on the bench. Two of her posse members suddenly appeared beside her.

Jimmy struggled to his feet and stared at Ginger Black and her friends in disbelief. Anger welled form deep within him, but he decided not to retaliate even though as far as he was concerned she had gone too far this time.

"Sax bothering you, Gin?" In the commotion Jimmy hadn't noticed football practice had ended and now Big Pete and Barry Spike were standing on the bench above them.

Jimmy scanned the assembled enemies as his patience reach the end. Arnold was nowhere to be seen. "Arnold, do your worse," he said under his breath.

Big Pete snorted derisively. "Listen to boner boy he thinks he's gonna take us on."

He slapped Barry's shoulder with the back of his hand.

Barry smirked. "Yeah, right." His eyes narrowed. "Let's teach this loser a lesson he'll never forget."

Suddenly Barry and Pete lifted off the ground as if they were puppets on strings into the air. It was as if gravity had suddenly disappeared. Their eyes went wide their mouths wide open trying to scream but nothing came out. The girls however managed to screeched in horror. "What're you doing?!" Ginger's eyes brimmed with fear and her usually pale complexion was pastier than ever.

Jimmy crossed his arms over his chest and grinned. "I'm not doing anything."

"Stop whatever it is right now!" his tormentor shouted at him.

The two football players floated away from the bleachers until they stopped moving to hover twenty feet above the playing field. A group of kids in the distance had starting running toward them drawn by the sight of two flying teenagers.

"If you stop bullying me I'll see what I can do." I hope Arnold's doing this.

"Yes, yes, of course. Just stop."

"Good." He paused and swallowed. "Arnold, release them."

The two terrified teenagers floated to the grass, after their shoes touched the ground, until they collapsed. Ginger and her friends squealed in delight then rushed down the bleachers and ran to them.

"It'll be worse next time if you break your promise," called Jimmy.

"Hey, bro, what the hell did you do?" Buddy had been with the group of kids running across the field.

Jimmy looked at his friend. "It was what I wanted to talk to you about...well sort of."

"You mean about your guardian angel?"

Jimmy froze. "You knew?"

Buddy smiled. "Yeah, of course, man. I have one too."

***

The next day in Mr. Wooldridge's class he discovered Ginger had asked to be in another teacher's history class meaning her reign of terror was finally over.

Though he knew he'd pay a price for the magic, he just hoped it wasn't too terrible. Shelly had even made a point of saying hello when he passed her in the hall this morning. Things would be different for him from now on.

"Hi, creep," said a voice behind him.

Turning in his seat he found Buddy looking back at him. Ginger was now in Buddy's former history class. Jimmy welcomed his friend with a grin.

Swiveling back in his seat to face front he noticed his angel sat perched on his right shoulder. Jimmy hadn't seen him since the incident at the playing field yesterday.

"I know you think I used magic on those boys," said Arthur.

"Who else would it be?" Jimmy whispered under his breath.

"I'm sure I have no idea," said Arthur his tiny feet moving across his shirt tickling him.

Jimmy considered his guardian angels response then dismissed any other explanation. Arthur had come to his rescue; it was the only logical explanation.

At least he hoped.

About the Author

International selling author, Russ Crossley, writes science fiction and fantasy, and mystery/suspense as well as their various subgenres.

His latest science fiction satire set in the far future, Revenge of the Lushites, is a sequel to Attack of the Lushites released in 2011. The latest title in the series was released in the fall of 2013. Both titles are available in e-book and trade paperback.

He has sold several short stories that have appeared in anthologies from various publishers including; WMG Publishing, Pocket Books, 53rd Street Publishing, and St. Martins Press.

He is a member of SF Canada and is past president of the Greater Vancouver Chapter of Romance Writers of America. He is also an alumni of the Oregon Coast Professional Fiction Writers Master Class taught by award winning author/editors, Kristine Katherine Rusch and Dean Wesley Smith.

Feel free to contact him on Facebook, Twitter, or his website http//:www.russcrossley.com. He loves to hear from readers.

Other titles by Russ Crossley you may enjoy
Razor and Edge Mysteries
The Kidnapping of Billy Buttons
String of Pearls
Death by Clown
Beggin' For Murder
Ragged Ice
The Grand Central Mystery
A Strange Case of Undead Murder

Jazz Stiletto Mysteries
A Day Without Sunshine
Skullduggery
Instrument of justice (first published in Over My Dead Body online mystery magazine)

The Amanda Dark paranormal mysteries
Hook Island
Grind Manor
Moonrise Diner
A Father's Daughter

The Trudy Wilson Mystery Novel Series
Bad Loyalty
Shear Murder
Buzzcut - coming soon

Other Novels

Attack of the Lushites
Revenge of the Lushites
My Zombie Prince
Antique Virgin
The Fire In Their Hearts
with R.S. Meger (from Champagne Books)
Zomopolis
The Last Serial Killer

Short Stories
Countdown
Shoeless Moe
Round Up At The Burger Bar:
The Story of Trixie Pug, Parts 1, 2, 3, 4, 5, 6, 7, 8, 9
Five Minutes
Blossom Queen, Barbarian
The Secret
The Family Line
End of the Flies
Death by Magic
The Penguin Sleeps With The Fishes
Only The Worthy
Hero For A Day
End of Empire
Strange Bedfellows
Big Business
A Perfect Crime
The Wise Guy and The Pirates
In Search of the Perfect Cup
T.I.N. Men
The Legend of G and the Dragonettes
The Incredible Mr. Fix-It
Lock Stock and Barrel
Divided Loyalties
Cave of Wonders
A Family Empire
Until We Meet Again
Dragon Rising
Solitary Man
The Keel Mountain Conspiracy
Angel on My Shoulder
Heroes of Old
The Great Bicycle Race
Tikka's Big Day
"My Partner the Zombie" —

Hungry For Your Love Anthology
(St. Martin's Press)
Big Hairy Deal
One Red Shoe
A Bad Day in Lunden Texas
Bloody Betty, Queen of the Pirates
Mirror Image
Dangerous Waters
Cape Disappointment
Boomerang
The Watcher of Wayburn Street
The Apprentice
Drip!
A Beautiful Friendship and The Parrot of Doom
Robine's Diary
The Christmas Club
Loose Ends
Splatter Pattern
It Takes Two
Lexicon
Replacement Parts
Sidekicks
Lost Stories
Time and Space
Survivors
Neighborhood Watch
Unnatural Immortal
Rum Runner's Lounge
It's A Small Galaxy
A Shattered Man
Betrayed
Replacement Parts
Clubhouse Heroes
Sounds That Angels Make
Muggins Rules – originally published in Fiction River Volume 12,
Risk Takers

Anthologies
Tales of Urban Fantasy
Five Tales of Bizarre Detectives
Tales of Mystery and Suspense
Tales of Weird Fantasy
Tales of Twisted Crime
Tales of The Unexpected
Tales From Space
10 by Russ Crossley
Round Up At The Burger Bar: The Story of Trixie Pug,
Parts 1- 5 The Beginning
Worlds of Science Fiction and Fantasy
More Tales of Mystery and Suspense
Justice Served
Love Stories
Ladies of the Jolly Roger with Rita Schulz
The Adventures of Razor and Edge:
Five Tales From The Quirky Detective Team
An Unexpected Journey
On Edge
Thrilling Adventures
Total War

Non-Fiction
The Writers Tools - The Synopsis

Also available from 53rd Street Publishing
http://www.53rdstreetpublishing.com

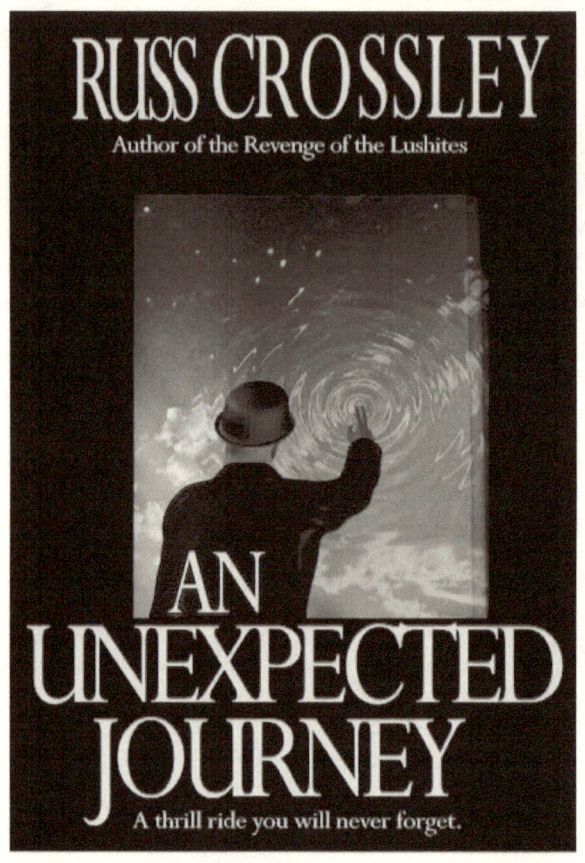

RUSS CROSSLEY

Author of the Revenge of the Lushites

AN
UNEXPECTED
JOURNEY

A thrill ride you will never forget.

Tales of alternate worlds where steam and alchemy mix during a race between empires, journey to a far off world on the other side of the galaxy where an ancient desperate struggle between good and evil is being fought. A story concerning a boy who has his own guardian angel. A story where you will discover a secret world hidden beneath our own where being odd is a virtue, and journey across the galaxy where an artificial intelligence decides the future of the human race.

Included in this volume is a new story about paranormal

investigator, Amanda Dark, and her continuing investigations into the dark corners of death where others fear to tread in the chilling tale, Moonrise Diner.

Check out this volume of extraordinary tales of mystery and the paranormal, these Unexpected Journey's

www.ingramcontent.com/pod-product-compliance
Lightning Source LLC
Chambersburg PA
CBHW021036130626
46552CB00005B/1878